Heather MacAllister
THE GOOD, THE BAD AND THE CUDDLY

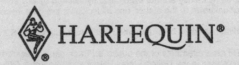

HARLEQUIN®

TORONTO • NEW YORK • LONDON
AMSTERDAM • PARIS • SYDNEY • HAMBURG
STOCKHOLM • ATHENS • TOKYO • MILAN • MADRID
PRAGUE • WARSAW • BUDAPEST • AUCKLAND

To fellow TCU alum Mary Ellen Deeves
Because it's about time I dedicated a book to her!

ISBN 0-373-25857-7

THE GOOD, THE BAD AND THE CUDDLY

Copyright © 1999 by Heather W. MacAllister.

This edition published by arrangement with Harlequin Books S.A.

Visit us at www.romance.net

Printed in U.S.A.

He was having a heart-to-heart with a baby!

Involuntarily, Steve looked around to see if anyone had overheard. Of course, in the locked storage unit, nobody was around but Maddie. Luckily, she was asleep, but it had been a close call.

He ought to give little Luke some advice—man-to-man information that his jerk of a father should have been around to give. Who knew what remained planted in a baby's subconscious until they could understand it?

"Okay, kid, listen up. I've got a few pieces of advice for you. Buy low, sell high, never stiff a waiter and change your oil every three thousand miles. Remember that it's fast cars and loose women, not loose cars and fast women. And never pay sticker price for either."

Luke actually stopped drinking from his baby bottle when Steve spoke. "Good, you're listening. Okay, let's talk about women. You don't hit them. Ever. And don't go giving your mom any lip, either. Tell her you love her and be a man—say it like you mean it." He glanced at Maddie, still asleep in the corner. "I know she's going to get on your nerves, 'cause she tends to get preachy, but she's a good woman."

And a good woman was the *last* thing he needed, Steve reminded himself. Especially an irritatingly sassy—and irresistibly sexy—woman like Maddie....

Dear Reader,

As a former music teacher, I've put on my share of Christmas pageants. And the first thing I learned was that the more "players" I had, the larger the captive audience of parents, families and friends.

However, one year I overdid it. *Nothing* had prepared me for the infamous "snowflake dance." (First-grade girls in white dresses draw LOTS of people). Since I was teaching in an area where there were a lot of shift workers, I had two casts—day and night. (We wouldn't want any parents to miss the chance of increasing the audience size, now, would we?) The daytime girls had so much fun, they showed up for the night performance, too. It was a blizzard—seventy-two little girls in white dresses whirled around the stage. Okay, what really happened was that seventy-two girls pushed and shoved, all trying to be in front so that their parents could take their picture on stage.

When writing *The Good, The Bad and the Cuddly,* you can bet I was remembering that play.

I wish you and yours a Merry Christmas!

Heather MacAllister

Books by Heather MacAllister

HARLEQUIN TEMPTATION
543—JILT TRIP
583—BEDDED BLISS
616—CHRISTMAS MALE
637—BRIDE OVERBOARD
656—LONG SOUTHERN NIGHTS
669—MANHUNTING IN MEMPHIS
711—MR. DECEMBER

1

NOT FINDING A parking place was seldom a life and death matter, but Maddie Givens was going to strangle somebody if she didn't find one soon. She was in that kind of mood.

She didn't want to be in that kind of mood. Good people didn't go ballistic because they couldn't find a parking place, even if their baby nephew was screaming his head off behind them in the backseat. And Maddie *did* want to be good. Truly.

And she tried. Really.

But she wasn't. Regrettably.

And nobody regretted that fact more than Maddie.

She wasn't cut out for the same kind of existence that her family was. Maddie craved adventure in her life—except her adventurous attempts had been as unsuccessful as her struggles to fit in with her family.

Life would be much simpler if Maddie felt the same desire to help her fellow human beings as her parents and sister.

Her sister had even found an equally virtuous man to marry. Maddie had found a husband, too—only he was already somebody else's, a fact he'd forgotten to mention.

Maddie couldn't help blaming herself. If she'd radiated goodness like Gloria, her sister, then the creep wouldn't have approached her. He'd obviously heard that little voice inside her calling out, "Maddie is a baddie."

So now, Maddie was trying harder than ever to live a life in selfless service to her fellow man.

Try to keep to the unmarried ones, this time, okay?

That wasn't fair, but the little voice inside her rarely was. All right then, she was *trying* to live a life in selfless service to her fellow human beings. And she would.

It would help if she were a good person, though.

Cars lined both sides of the street in front of the East Street Community Center. If Maddie were truly as good as her parents, who ran the center, she'd be thankful that so many people had turned out for the Christmas pageant dress rehearsal this evening. That was the good way to look at the situation.

Instead, she wanted to jump out of her car and let the air out of the tires of the shiny black car that was taking up two choice parking places in front of the center's thrift shop.

Behind her, Luke, her nephew, continued to wail in his car seat. As much as Maddie loved Luke—and all her nephews—at this precise moment, she wanted to love him from a distance.

His crying was so loud it nearly drowned out the clanking of an engine badly in need of a tune-up. But after a car had been driven a hundred and fifty-seven thousand miles, something was bound to clank, especially since the carburetor was unenthusiastically providing whatever it was that carburetors were supposed to provide. At least she had a car, such as it was. She should be grateful.

Maddie concentrated on thinking grateful thoughts, but with Luke wailing for all he was worth, it was hard to hear herself think.

Maybe it was just as well that she couldn't find a parking place immediately. Gloria always insisted that driving made Luke sleepy.

Maddie knew that Gloria would never lie. However, in this case, her sister was clearly in denial. Since she was currently bedridden with the flu, no doubt contracted from volunteering at the center's clinic, Maddie decided to cut her some slack.

But she only had enough patience to cut slack for Gloria, not the jerk taking up two parking spots.

Maddie slowed her car. Farther down the block, the line for the evening meal at the soup kitchen stretched almost to the corner. Nobody was paying any attention to her. She could just hop out, give the valve stem a twist and...

He was still there. She sensed him watching her even before her gaze slid across the street to the man who occupied Casa Garcia's prime patio table. Something within Maddie sighed, the part of her that she wished wouldn't notice broad shoulders, slim hips, and an attractively beard-roughened jaw before it knew anything about the man within.

Regrettably, that part of Maddie didn't care a whole lot about the man within when the package was so intriguing.

He'd come into the center a couple of days ago. She'd found him in the rec room when she'd been carting in the sets for the Christmas pageant. He'd looked so out of place and so... She exhaled. He was the kind of man to make a woman wish she was wearing something tight and red and slit up to there instead of dowdy and denim and down to the floor. Not that Maddie owned something tight in red, or any other color.

A car behind her honked and Maddie stomped on the accelerator, which sent her car into a jerking fit that renewed Luke's crying.

"Hush, little Luuuuke," she crooned. "Please?"

He did not hush.

"What's up?" She gazed at him in the rearview mirror. "You've just been fed, so you can't fool me into thinking you're hungry. Remember burping on Aunt Maddie's blouse? That was lots of fun, wasn't it?"

And Gloria had insisted on dragging herself out of her sickbed to wash Maddie's blouse leaving Maddie with no choice but to wrap herself in the robes of Gloria's Mary costume. But it was okay. Maddie was running late, and this way she wouldn't have to take time to change into the costume later.

There. That was a positive way to look at the situation, wasn't it?

Luke snuffled. He'd long ago tossed his pacifier out of both his and Maddie's reach, and now stuffed his fingers into his mouth. His eyelids drooped. Maybe he *was* only sleepy.

At least he'd finally stopped crying.

As she drove slowly down the street, Maddie smiled at the people in the soup kitchen line, hoping that they'd think she looked serene and good. She was already dressed as the serenest person in history, wasn't she?

Faking serenity was good practice for later when

she had to shepherd a dozen of her kindergarten sheep during the rehearsal *and* take Gloria's place as Mary in the pageant. Maddie secretly hoped some of that serenity and goodness would rub off on her. Either Mary's or Gloria's would be okay. Frankly, it was hard to tell them apart.

Maddie reached the end of the block and scooted through a yellow light to turn the corner. Maybe she'd find a parking spot on this next pass around the block.

The trunk was full of lamb costumes, as well as angel wings and the crowns for the three kings. Flu or not, Gloria was still the glue-gun queen. Now, Maddie had to carry all this stuff and Luke, the star of the show, inside the center for tonight's rehearsal.

These were good and noble objectives, so was it too much to ask for a parking place?

Apparently so.

STEVE JACKSON STARED at his third meal in a row of Casa Garcia's green chili burritos and wondered if he should have buffered the assault on his stomach with breakfast—a bland oatmeal kind of breakfast that would have stayed with him throughout the day. Not a three-cups-of-instant-coffee breakfast.

That wasn't to say that Mama Garcia's burritos, tamales, chalupas and her own fiery salsa weren't some of the best Tex-Mex he'd ever eaten. But years of knocking back countless cups of coffee had rusted a few holes in his cast-iron stomach.

He rubbed the stubble on his face and shifted on the uncomfortable patio chair outside the tiny café. If he had to change to decaf now, he might as well hang up the property recovery business.

Actually, he could afford to hang it up any time he wanted to.

The thing was, he didn't want to. Ever. Even though it meant more stakeouts like the one he was on now. Steve didn't like stakeouts.

He *enjoyed* outwitting insurance cheats, though strictly speaking, he left the crooks to the police and the assorted law-enforcement agencies who were always grateful to hear a tip from him. His business was to find and recover property on which the insurance agency had paid a claim.

He specialized in cases where the leads had grown cold, and everyone else had given up. A Jackson case was synonymous with all-but-unsolvable. He was the last resort. The heavy artillery. Insurance companies had been known to close files if he refused to take the case. He didn't refuse many.

Though he relished the expression on people's faces when they knew they'd been caught, he never indulged himself at the expense of the property. That came first, along with a twelve percent finder's fee.

Ten percent of that was standard recovery pay. The extra two percent was because he could get it.

Yeah, when the time came, he'd miss the assets recovery game and the feeling of satisfaction that came with a successful conclusion. But not this sitting-around-and-waiting-for-something-to-break garbage. He liked action. He liked to stay on the move. Stakeouts gave him too much time to think. Steve didn't like thinking about his life and what it was—or wasn't.

During this case, in which he'd followed a couple of petty thieves recently released from prison, he'd done way too much thinking. The twinges in his stomach were just little hints that he wasn't as young as he used to be. Eventually the time would come when he could no longer chase down criminals—literally and figuratively.

He didn't want to think about that.

Instead, he studied his dinner, then tilted the oval plastic plate so that the orange grease drained into a well he'd made in the refried beans. After trapping the grease behind a dam of beans, he glanced over at the East Street Community Center and Shelter. Lots of activity going on over there.

Rumor had it they were serving meat loaf and mashed potatoes tonight. The meat loaf and mashed potatoes called to him and it looked like it called to a fair number of Houston's homeless and hungry as well. It was going on five-thirty and the line outside the soup kitchen already stretched halfway down the block.

If he hadn't wanted to avoid being seen by Frank and Murray, the two yo-yos he was after, Steve would have joined the line.

Lunch's burrito still sat in his stomach, right under the tamales and queso chaser he'd ordered about three. Mama Garcia wasn't inclined to question why an unshaven biker chose to spend the whole day occupying one of her patio tables as long as said biker kept ordering food and drink.

This wasn't an area of Houston where a man, even a man who looked as scruffy as he did, would leave a restored classic Harley unattended, so Mama Garcia's patio suited Steve just fine.

As the day lengthened, he increased the tips, and nobody bothered the black-clad man with the book. Now, it was dusk and even with the multicolored Christmas lights blinking in time to "Feliz Navidad," he couldn't fake reading any longer.

What a way to spend a holiday. Not that Christmas to him was anything other than a Saturday this year—an annoying extra holiday during the weekend when everything would shut down, making it harder for him to get his job done. He stood and shoved the paperback he'd been reading about the wreck of the *Maria Elena* into the pack on the back of his bike and returned to the table.

As he dug into the burrito, a battered red Honda with a blue door passed by for the second time in the past few minutes, one of a number of vehicles in the five o'clock exodus from downtown. Steve had noticed it because of the blue door and wondered if Frank and Murray were driving it, casing the community center.

He knew they'd been hanging around the center— that's why *he'd* been hanging around. The two new ex-cons might only be interested in the soup kitchen, or the thrift shop, or a warm bed for the night. It made sense and Steve was beginning to think that his instinct had let him down. Maybe it was getting rusty, same as his stomach.

If they were driving the Honda, they weren't acting like two crooks who'd recently fenced gold doubloons worth a couple hundred thousand dollars. They weren't smart enough to put him off the trail, so either they hadn't recovered the doubloons everyone thought they'd hidden after the theft three years ago, or they'd actually told the truth for once and hadn't stolen them.

Or they were smarter than he thought.

No.

These were the idiots who'd waved to the hotel security camera before smashing it, evidently not realizing there would be a videotape, he reminded himself.

"Señor?" A middle-aged woman set down flour tortillas sandwiched between two plates.

Steve looked up. In the doorway behind the woman stood a man with a paunch, probably her husband. Behind him was a younger man, no paunch, trying to look threatening and doing a credible job.

"The café will be closing early tonight," she announced.

Here it comes, Steve thought. They were getting ready to kick him out. Mama Garcia's hadn't done much business today and the Garcia clan had evidently decided that potential customers didn't want to walk by Steve.

He couldn't blame them. He knew how he looked—black denim, black leather, purposefully developed muscles and a don't-mess-with-me demeanor that was designed to discourage casual conversation.

"You are welcome to sit here as long as you like, but if you want more food or coffee, you must order it now."

Steve glanced at the two men behind her and shook his head. "I'm fine, thanks."

Mama Garcia withdrew a notepad, ripped off the top sheet and placed the check facedown by his plate. A cheerful "Gracías!" was penciled on the back.

To his surprise, she lingered. "It's gonna get cold out here now that the sun has gone down. We're going to be across the street at the center for the Christmas pageant rehearsal. Me, I'm in the choir and my granddaughter is a little lamb."

Her husband said something in Spanish. Steve only knew enough Spanish to catch the gist of it, but even if he hadn't, he'd known the man was hurrying her along.

He reached for his wallet and pulled out a twenty. "I don't need change."

Mama Garcia made a clucking sound. "Too much."

"It's okay."

Muttering, she left, then returned some minutes later with a container of food. "Since you like my burritos so much," she explained.

Steve nodded and exercised his smile muscles. They never got much of a workout. "The dishes?" He gestured to the plastic plate and glass.

"Leave 'em. And maybe later you'll come across the street. You'd be welcome if..." she shrugged. "If you think that's some place you'd like to go."

In other words, if he needed a bed for the night. He started to make a noncommittal remark, then changed his mind. "Who runs the place?" He already knew the bare facts about the center and the peacenik couple who ran it, but it never hurt to hear another version.

"Brother and Sister Givens and their family." Mama Garcia kissed her fingers and gestured skyward. "They are saints."

Probably saints with an agenda.

Steve wondered how Mama Garcia could think so highly of folks who were giving away food right across the street from her café.

Maybe she was a saint, too. He already knew she could cook like an angel.

"They sure feed a lot of people—where do they get the kind of money it takes to run that place?" It wouldn't be the first time a thrift shop had been the cover for a fencing operation.

An instant chill surrounded him. "Those of us who have, give to those who do not have," Mama Garcia snapped.

Sounded like a sore subject. Maybe he wasn't the first to ask questions. However, Steve didn't want her mad in case he had to park himself here again tomorrow. Indicating the extra food she'd given him, he said, "I imagine people are as generous as you this time of year."

She thawed, but her nod was tight before she turned and went back inside.

Interesting reaction. Was it possible that the good Brother Givens was fencing on the side and the community was turning a blind eye?

It would take some doing to find the right buyer for the gold doubloons. Antiquity wise, they were far more valuable than for their gold content. He'd been keeping tabs on the activities of known collectors, but so far, no one had shifted any money, or taken any sudden trips. There'd been no ripples in the murky waters of the antiquities underground.

When the street had been quiet this afternoon, Steve had read about the shipwreck from which the doubloons had been recovered. Interesting story, but nothing of special historical significance that would add to their value. They'd just been intended as the dowry of an unfortunate Mexican bride.

He wondered if the guy had married her anyway.

Nice custom, that paying the groom to get married business. They ought to revive it. Steve knew that the only way *he'd* ever get married again was if he were paid.

Yeah, he'd done suburbia and suburbia had nearly done him in.

That had been a real shock. He'd finally managed to get the kind of life he'd always wanted, then found he didn't know how to live it.

He crammed a forkful of burrito into his mouth. He was thinking again. That was the trouble with stakeouts. Too much time to think.

If he was going to think about anything, he should think about Frank and Murray.

He must be missing something with them. There was the chance they'd been working for somebody, but when they'd been offered the usual squeal deals, they hadn't taken them, which was unusual for small-time thieves in their position. Prison records indicated that there hadn't been anyone contacting them except a couple of their friends and Murray's grandmother.

Steve had checked out both the grandmother and

the friends. Nothing there. Ditto for the hotel house-keeping staff.

The claimant who'd owned the doubloons had disappeared shortly after the theft and the insurance company payment. Their investigators had come up dry, but the doubloons had to be somewhere. If something didn't shake loose soon, Steve was going to have to go back to the hotel and take the room apart, even if it had been nearly three years since the theft. It wouldn't be the first time something reported stolen had later been found to have fallen behind furniture.

He scanned the soup-kitchen line again, searching for the two men. Frank was short, dark, and furtive, but Murray was a tall, lanky guy with a goofy expression and had recently taken to wearing a safety-orange knit cap. Nobody could blend in a crowd with that cap. It was an old trick—get anyone following you used to looking for something distinctive you were wearing, then give it to somebody else and hope it was a while before the switch was noticed.

Steve considered taking up Mama Garcia's suggestion and going over to the center tonight. He'd already explored the place, had, in fact, eaten lunch at the soup kitchen a couple of days ago. A real nice bowl of chili—no beans—over rice. He'd skipped the green gelatin salad, but had grabbed an apple on the way out.

The thrift store next door was mostly clothing and furniture castoffs. The blond babe working there had informed him that toys were in short supply due to the season, but if he had a real need for Christmas toys, to put his name on a list and she'd see what she could do. Her smile was so sweet and so bright, that he'd mumbled something and left immediately.

Though he didn't want to admit it, the encounter with her had rattled him. She wasn't just a blonde, she radiated blond, blue-eyed goodness. As he gazed into those blue eyes, for just a second, he'd felt as though she glowed with a light that could brighten even the dark corners of his heart.

That kind of goodness unnerved him, so he left as fast as he could without looking suspicious. He stepped across the hall and found himself in a recreation room with a basketball goal. Idly, he picked up a well-worn ball from the plastic toy-filled crates stacked against the wall, dribbled a couple of times, then took a shot. The ball bounced off the rim and the metal twang echoed in the empty room.

Just couldn't get it right. The story of his life.

"May I help you?"

Steve whirled around to find a woman standing just inside the doorway, her arms full of long rolls of painted paper.

It wasn't the blonde.

Or rather not the same glowing blonde. This woman watched him warily, seeing straight into his black heart, all right, but there was nothing illuminating about her gaze.

He was almost relieved. "I was just..." Under her stare, he trailed off and gestured toward the basketball goal.

She walked a few feet into the room and her gaze swept over him. "Volunteering to help build sets for the Christmas pageant as a way to express your thanks for the nutritious, filling, and, oh yes, *free* lunch you just ate?" Standing the rolls of paper against the side wall, she left before he could reply.

Steve blinked, then blinked again. So she liked to dish out a little guilt with the charity. This was definitely *not* the other blonde. He chucked the basketball into its crate and dug into his pocket, coming up with a ten-dollar bill.

He found her dragging four-by-eight pieces of cardboard down the hallway.

"Here." He thrust the ten at her.

She looked from it to his face and he thought she might have even blushed a little. "We don't charge for meals here."

Right. "If there's one thing I've learned in this world, it's that there's no such thing as a free lunch." A can halfway filled with coins sat on a shelf by the coatrack. Steve stuffed his money inside.

"That's the cussing can," she told him.

"It was a *damn* good bowl of chili," he said, and walked out.

The woman had been sassier than anyone wearing a long baggy dress and flat shoes had a right to be. And she'd checked him out—she'd definitely checked him out. He would have returned the favor, except in that dress, there wasn't much to check. Yet now, as Steve contemplated paying another visit to the center, he knew he was more interested in seeing her again than the knockout blonde.

Not that he had anything against seeing the blonde—

A bright orange blob appeared in the soup kitchen line.

Murray still wore the hat. Next to him, Frank,

hands shoved into his pockets, shifted nervously from foot to foot, managing to look suspicious even while waiting for free food.

The Garcias had turned off the music before they left, so now their Christmas lights burned steadily, not only keeping Steve visible, but making it hard for him to see out into the darkness.

He ate slowly, just for show now, and watched Frank and Murray's progress in line. As soon as they reached the kitchen door, he'd slip into the shadows next to his bike.

Frank began gesturing as Murray shook his head. Steve squinted, but the damn lights made it hard to see. Easing off the metal chair, he stood slowly, not wanting his movements to attract their attention.

Frank pointed and Murray shook his head again, and was still shaking it when Frank shoved him. With obvious reluctance, Murray ambled out of line.

Oh, great. They were splitting up.

The Honda chugged by again and this time double-parked by the center's main entrance, leaving the motor running.

A woman wearing a robed costume got out of the car and released the bungee cord holding the trunk closed. She grabbed an armful of something white and gold and walked hurriedly across the sidewalk to the center's glass door.

She was having trouble negotiating both her costume and the door, and Steve saw that nobody gave up his place in line to help her. *Jerks,* he thought.

She eventually dumped the stuff just inside the door, came back out and grabbed another load from the trunk about the time Murray ambled up. She stopped, clearly asking him to help her and he obligingly relieved her of her load of beige woolly-looking fabric. Turning back to the car, she looped three gold crowns around her arm and grabbed a couple of brown grocery sacks. Murray returned and she said something to him over her shoulder. At that moment, Frank stalked down the street.

"You moron! What do you think you're doing?" His voice carried clearly in the cool evening air.

"He's just helping me." The woman raised her voice as well.

"He doesn't need to be helpin' nobody! He's got stuff to do." Frank gave him a shove. "You've got stuff to do."

"Aw, Frank—"

"Go on!"

Murray looked helplessly from Frank to the woman.

"Excuse me, we're talking thirty seconds here," she said. "Less, if you help."

What light there was caught her full in the face just then and Steve recognized her as the woman he'd met in the rec room the other day. The darker blond one. The interesting one.

"I ain't helpin' and neither's he." Frank stepped toward Murray, who flinched.

"Leave him alone," she ordered in a tone that was used to being obeyed.

"Lady, this doesn't concern you."

Steve had to agree with him, even as he admired her guts.

Frank grabbed Murray's arm and attempted to hustle him down the sidewalk.

She was a lone woman on a street in an iffy part of Houston. The smart thing to do would be to go on inside. But Steve had already figured out that she wasn't the meekly retiring sort.

Sure enough, she marched back to the car just as Frank pushed Murray again. He stumbled and stepped on her costume. She tripped, dropping an armful of what Steve knew were props and costumes for the Christmas pageant.

There was a thud, then the unmistakable sound of pottery breaking.

"Look what you did! My sister painted that!"

"Then your sister can paint another one!" Frank kicked at the broken pieces.

"Stop it! What's the matter with you?"

He raised his arm.

Everything happened in slow motion for Steve as a sickening feeling that had nothing to do with too many burritos invaded his stomach.

Frank was going to hit the woman and she didn't even realize it. She didn't flinch, didn't cower, and didn't give ground.

"Stop!" Steve roared from too far away. "You hit her and I'll hit you!"

Everyone froze momentarily to stare at him.

Murray pointed. "Hey, that's the guy on the motorcy—"

"Get in the car!" Frank lunged past the woman and yanked open the door. For once, Murray complied without question.

Steve swore and took off for his motorcycle. Double-parked with the motor running. What had she been thinking?

He could hear her outraged tirade as the doors slammed and the engine revved.

He shoved on his helmet hoping she wasn't going to do anything stupid—even more stupid than she already had—like hanging on the door handle as Frank drove away. She was mostly yelling and beating on the window, but she wasn't hanging, he saw with relief.

The Honda took off and so did Steve.

"Somebody stop them!" she yelled.

He swung by, intending to reassure her. The car wasn't any great loss, but he wasn't going to say that.

Pulling alongside the curb he shouted, "I'm going after them!"

"I'm coming with you." And then she latched onto the bike.

"No, you're not."

But she gathered her skirts and swung her leg over.

"Hey!" Steve jammed his foot against the pavement as her weight tilted the bike. "Get off!"

"No!"

"Look, just calm down, go back inside, and put on your little Christmas play."

She glared at him. "That's going to be tricky since they just drove off with the baby who's playing Jesus!"

2

Now *THAT* was an attention getter. "You mean—"

"Didn't you hear me? There's a *baby* in that car!" She twisted around. "Where's your passenger helmet?"

"I don't take passengers. *Get off the bike.*" Usually that tone was enough to attract the attention of the person to whom it was directed.

Ignoring both Steve and his tone, she grabbed so tightly around his waist that he gasped. "I'm ready—get going!"

"It'll be faster my way."

"Now where have I heard *that* before?" she muttered. "Quit arguing and move it!"

The whole exchange had taken less than ten seconds, but it was enough time for Frank and Murray to turn the corner. It was now or never and Steve had been waiting too long for it to be never. "Hang on."

Of course, she already was and in a way that told him she was no novice rider.

The motorcycle roared away from the curb. In the rearview mirror, Steve noticed that the people in the soup kitchen line were just watching blankly. Probably no one had alerted the center's staff to call for help. Actually, he wouldn't mind having the police stay out of this one until he had a chance to question Frank and Murray in person.

As he leaned into the corner Steve was aware of just how *very* long it had been since a woman had wrapped her arms around his waist and pressed herself next to him on his bike.

Or anywhere else.

Her body felt good against his, and the fact that he noticed while he was in the middle of a pursuit was unsettling. One more thing for him to think about later when he didn't want to be thinking.

Her robes flapped behind them creating enough drag to make the engine crank up a few more rpms, but he had the stolen, mostly red Honda in view once again.

When she saw the car, she relaxed her hold marginally, and melted against him, shifting her body weight when he did, keeping her head down. Keeping quiet.

She was good. She'd be worth taking on a long ride sometime when he wasn't on the job.

Sometime when she wasn't married with a kid.

He briefly envied her unknown husband until he remembered what marriage had been like—and that was without a kid.

No thanks.

The end-of-the-day traffic was still heavy, but he could maneuver between cars and lanes, and Frank, who was driving, couldn't. Taking advantage, Steve worked his way toward the car until he was about three vehicles back.

As soon as the signal changed he stayed with the traffic until the next block when it looked like he was going to get caught by a red light. He made his way directly behind the Honda.

Inside the car, Murray turned and saw them, but then his eyes grew huge and he went slack-jawed.

If Steve had to guess, he'd say Murray had just discovered the baby.

Murray grabbed Frank's arm causing the car to swerve. Frank shook him off, his lips moving as he undoubtedly bawled out Murray.

The light turned yellow while Frank was still yelling. When he faced forward again, he was moving too fast to stop and ran the light as it turned red.

Steve heard the gasp behind him. If she hadn't been there, he would have run the light, too.

He hit the brakes.

"What are you *doing?* They'll get away!"

"Light's red."

"So? Traffic hadn't started moving. You could have made it!"

So? *So?*

If that's the way she wanted it… "Fine."

With a roar, he popped the clutch, and peeled across three lanes of traffic, ran up on the sidewalk, cut through a gas station parking lot, pulled a U-turn, hit the intersection again, and turned right.

Not a peep from behind.

He felt his beard brush against the helmet pads as he smiled.

Then… "That's more like it! For a minute there, I thought you were all show and no go."

Incredible. Unbelievable. And pretty damn irritating. Obviously, the only way she'd managed to survive in the world this long was sheer dumb luck and he couldn't afford to get crosswise with that kind of luck. As someone once said, the only kind of luck he'd had was bad luck.

Besides, he kind of admired her guts, like a mother bear after her cub. If his own mother had possessed even half of what this woman had, maybe she could have stood up to his father. Maybe his childhood would have been something other than a series of screaming alcoholic fights, beatings, hiding out, and moving every time the military transferred them.

And maybe it wouldn't have been.

The car suddenly turned from the center lane, leaving angry honking in its wake.

"Damn." Steve barely whispered, but the wind must have carried the word back to her.

"Why? What's wrong?"

He waited until they'd turned before answering and then he was careful not to use names. "They're not going to take the freeway out of town—they just cut southeast. They're heading toward the ship channel."

"Is that bad?"

"Lots of hiding places down there."

She said nothing more because there was nothing more to be said. He gave her points for realizing it.

He hoped she'd thrown a few good thoughts his way, too. If reuniting a mother and child wasn't worth some major cosmic points, then he didn't know what was.

But they hadn't been reunited, yet. As he and the woman left downtown Houston, the streetlights became more infrequent, especially once they turned off Navigation. Night had fallen and the area they traveled through now was mostly industrial with narrow, nearly deserted streets. An occasional string of Christmas lights broke the halogen glow from the parking lots they sped past. The Honda ignored all stop signs and traffic signals to the point of worrying even Steve. Crashing themselves up was one thing, but Frank and Murray had a baby in the car.

He thought of the woman clinging to him. She must be scared out of her wits. He wished he could reassure her, but he wasn't all that sure how this episode was going to turn out, himself.

Warehouse row loomed ahead of them and beyond that, the docks and the channel itself. The Honda was going to have to make a move soon, or end up in the water.

Frank must have realized the same thing. Tires squealing, the car suddenly turned into a commercial warehouse rental place.

By the time Steve reached the driveway and buzzed through the open gates, the Honda was out of sight, having disappeared down one of the dozens of alleys leading between the individual storage units.

The place was like a maze. Steve slowed his bike to a crawl. "You look to the right, I'll take the left."

"Okay." She shivered, though whether from cold or fear, Steve didn't know.

She was entitled to both. Though it wasn't very cold, she wasn't wearing a coat and riding around on the back of a motorcycle without one would have been chilling.

They slowly crept down the main drive, but had seen no sign of the Honda when they'd reached the chain-link fence at the back of the property. That meant the car had stopped somewhere and had turned off the engine. Great.

Steve maneuvered between the end units and looked down the alley. Nothing. Reversing, he checked the line of units on the right. Still nothing.

"Hear the car?" he asked his passenger.

"No." He felt her shake her head.

But they were there, watching. He sensed it.

Acting on a hunch, Steve revved the motor and headed back toward the entrance. At the last minute, he turned and followed the fence line, reducing his speed until he stopped, hoping it would sound as though he'd driven away.

Turning off the motor, he held his finger to his lips, then gestured the woman off the bike. She looked at him questioningly, but did as he asked. Steve walked his bike to the far side of the rental office out of sight of the storage units. Once there, he got back on the bike and gestured for her to do so as well.

Before she did, she looked him full in the face, her gaze assessing. He'd let her assess all she wanted, just as long as she didn't start jabbering.

As a matter of fact, Steve did a little assessing, himself. Now that he was face to face with her, he could see her resemblance to the blonde in the thrift shop. Sisters, unless he missed his guess. But they didn't have a whole lot else in common. She was prettier than he'd remembered, even though she was narrowing her eyes at him.

Steve felt a flicker of awareness that could grow into a full-fledged tail-wagging unless he consciously put a stop to it.

She stopped it for him. Bending forward, she asked in the barest of whispers, "Do you know what you're doing?"

It was a little late in the day for second thoughts, but Steve understood. She was a woman alone with a stranger in a part of town where no woman wanted to be out alone after dark. Two bozos had just stolen her car with her baby inside. Under the circumstances, she was remarkably calm, and he admired her for it.

So he gave her his most reassuring expression. "Yes. I know what I'm doing."

He thought about showing her his ID, but with his luck, that would be the moment Frank and Murray made a run for the entrance, so he held her gaze until she satisfied some inner criteria of hers and climbed back onto the bike.

He was pleased she trusted him. As his ears strained to hear the car's distinctively rough engine, Steve wondered what she'd seen in him. Based on outward appearances alone, he wouldn't trust *himself*.

"Don't you think we ought—"

Steve held up a hand and she shut up, but he heard her exhale in frustration.

After that, she was quiet, which kind of surprised him. So far, she hadn't taken direction all that well.

The sounds of the night settled around them—the buzz of the security lights, and distant metallic echoes as cranes unloaded cargo and forklifts carried it away from the dock. Here and there, a mournful diesel horn sounded as a ship glided in the channel.

A car door slammed and an engine badly in need of a tune-up turned over.

That was it. "Hold on tight." Steve listened until he could determine the direction the car was moving, then stomped on the accelerator and took off with the throttle wide open.

The sound of the car was about midway down the line of storage units to the left. Frank and Murray were moving toward the gate. He cut in between the buildings to head them off and roared down the alley. If all went well, the Honda wouldn't be driving past at the exact moment he emerged from the alley, which could get messy.

He braced himself and shot out into the open immediately looking for the car.

"There it is!" Her arm appeared in his side vision as she pointed.

At first he didn't see the car, then noticed a dark hulk at the far end by the back fence. One door hung open.

Under other circumstances, he would have taken time to look around more, but the she-bear behind him was pounding his shoulder and shouting "Go!" in his ear.

So Steve went, his wheels spitting gravel against the metal buildings.

He skidded to a halt and wobbled as she scrambled to get off the bike. "Hey, wait!"

But she ignored him to run to the car and stick her head in the open door.

"Luke!" Her body sagged for an instant, then she pushed the seat forward and leaned inside.

Steve exhaled. So the kid was still in there and

Frank and Murray had taken off. They were finally showing some smarts. They'd obviously figured that Steve wasn't going to stop chasing them while they had the baby and that kidnapping wouldn't look too good to their parole officers.

Steve got off the bike and walked over to the car. "Is he okay?"

"Shh!"

Incredibly, it seemed as though the kid had slept through the whole thing. The woman fiddled with his blankets and stroked his head as she murmured mushy baby things.

"Did they leave the keys?" Steve asked.

She pushed back the pale blue hood of her costume and glared at him. "I wasn't looking for the keys. I was looking for Luke." Turning back to the baby, she rubbed her finger over the top of his head.

Steve stood there watching them. Mother and child, together again. How touching.

"You're welcome," he said caustically.

Without looking at him, she exhaled. "I suppose you want a reward."

"I don't need a reward." He glanced at the ignition and didn't see the keys. Swell. "I *expected* a little gratitude, but I don't need that either."

"I do appreciate what you—"

"Save it."

He checked the floor mats and seats, then stooped to look under the car in case Frank had dropped or thrown the keys.

A mistake. One of several he'd made recently, but by far the most painful.

There was the scrape of a shoe, a yelping gasp

quickly muffled, then Steve was whacked in the head, fortunately by somebody who didn't quite know what he was doing.

The edges of his vision darkened, but he didn't lose consciousness as he slumped to his knees. For a fraction of an instant, he thought the woman might have hit him. From what he knew of her, she seemed more than capable.

"Ow! She bit me!" Murray howled.

He should have known Frank and Murray wouldn't have abandoned the car to run on foot.

A scream shredded the night.

Steve allowed his body to drop to the pavement, feigning unconsciousness to give his head time to clear. Faking wasn't hard. It looked like a string of Christmas lights had exploded behind his eyelids. Felt like it too.

"Let me go!" There were sounds of a struggle.

"Keep her quiet!"

"She'll bite me!"

"Tell him to get his filthy hands off me! It's not like I'm going to run off and leave the baby here."

Frank stepped over Steve's body. "Shut up, lady, or I'll hit you, too!"

"I'm surprised you haven't already."

"Look, I got no beef with you—"

"And you do with him?"

Steve sensed them all looking at him. He kept his breathing even.

"He's been spying on us," Murray whined.

"Shut *up*, Murray, or I'll bean *you*."

"Why do you think he's been spying on you?" she asked.

Would it kill her to ask if she could see if he was okay?

"We saw him."

"*Everybody* has seen him hanging around Mama Garcia's the past couple of days. That doesn't mean he's spying on you. He's probably down on his luck and has too much pride to ask for help. You two obviously have no pride. You've been getting free handouts for nearly a week and I have yet to see either of you in chapel."

"Is that where they hide the dessert?" Murray asked.

"Idiot."

"Actually, yes, we serve cookies and sometimes cakes and pies after evening devotional. It was cake tonight." Her voice lowered. "Chocolate cake."

"Chocolate cake?" Murray asked wistfully.

"Mmm, yes. Chocolate cake with chocolate fudge frosting—and it's only two days old this time. The bakery wanted to make room for the Christmas pumpkin pie orders."

"Hey, Frank, could we—"

There was a muffled thud.

"Stop picking on him!"

Above their voices, Steve heard another sound, fitful at first, then with gathering steam.

The baby was awake.

"Now look what you've done!" With a swish of robes, the woman hurried to the car.

One little peep from the kid and there she was. But did she spare a thought for Steve, her knight in gleaming leather?

"What's the matter with you two? Just go away and leave us alone."

"And give you a chance to call the police?" Frank asked. "No way."

"I'm sure the police were called long ago," she said with a confidence Steve didn't share. "Even with your tiny brains, you can tell that I'm in costume. Tonight is the Christmas pageant rehearsal. Considering the parts we're playing, it's not like they won't notice we're gone."

Her robes brushed Steve's face as she sat in the car and cooed to the baby. "Hi sweetie. Did the bad men scare you?"

"Oh, Frank, we're in big trouble. She's...she's... and he's...he's—"

"Shut up and let me think."

How could anybody think with the baby crying? Steve risked opening his eyes a sliver. It was about time for him to make a move and he wanted to know everyone's location. Ideally, if he could find a way to let the woman know to lock herself in the car, then he wouldn't have to worry about her interfering as he took out Frank and Murray.

He couldn't see anything with her robes in the way. But that meant that Frank and Murray couldn't see him all that well, either.

He was just about to whisper to her when the sound of the baby's crying changed as she took him out of his car seat and held him against her shoulder. Within a few moments, the crying stopped and Steve felt cool fingers search at his neck for a pulse. She sighed when she found one.

"Don't you know that no good deed goes unpunished?" she whispered as her fingers lingered, exploring the back of his head and brushing the hair away from his temple.

Her touch was unexpectedly comforting and her words were so in tune with his own feelings, that Steve was stopped cold, and the opportunity to signal her passed.

"Hey, you—Mary," Frank called.

"My name is Maddie," she corrected.

Maddie. If felt strange to be able to put a name to her. Maddie. He'd never known a Maddie, but he wouldn't have picked her for one. She was more like a Brunhilde.

"Whoever you are, get away from him."

"He needs a doctor." She stood. "He's still unconscious and there's blood all over the back of his head."

Damn. Blood stains were a bear to get out.

"Look...Maddie." Frank heaved a sigh. "Murray and me, we don't want any trouble."

"No, no trouble," Murray echoed.

"It's a little late for that," she snapped.

Quiet, Maddie.

Lucky for her, Frank ignored her crack. "The thing is, Murray and me have been looking for something of ours. We think you might have it in that thrift shop where you work."

"Yeah, my grandmother, she, like, donated all my stuff when I, when I—"

"When he was away," Frank continued smoothly.

"And you want it back?"

"Yeah."

Steve practically stopped breathing in order to

hear what was being said. This was it. Murray must have been hiding the doubloons at his grandmother's house in something that she gave away.

"When did your grandmother make her donation?" Maddie asked, swaying from side to side as she held the baby.

With each sway, the hem of her costume brushed his head.

"I dunno." There was a more than a hint of desperation in Murray's voice and Steve guessed that Frank had given him a lot of grief over this. "She moved into that home last year, so I guess that's when she gave my stuff away."

"*Last year?*" The swaying stopped. "Have you already looked in the thrift shop?"

"Kinda."

"Well, if you didn't see anything of yours, then the things are probably gone by now."

"Gone where?"

"Sold or given away—that's what happens to merchandise in a thrift shop."

"Do you know who you sold it to?" Frank asked.

"It could have been anybody. I don't even know what you're talking about. We get things all year long—"

"Don't you people keep records? What kind of place are you runnin'?"

Steve could hear the agitation in Frank's voice and subtly shifted his weight so he'd be ready to intervene if necessary.

"My father runs an *honest* place! I'll have you know that there are extremely meticulous records. I set them up, myself. We have to keep them in order to maintain our nonprofit status."

"Wait a minute—the preacher is your old man?" Frank asked.

Say no. Say you meant Father Givens.

"Yes, Pastor Givens is my father."

Big mistake, Maddie.

The tone of Frank's voice changed. "And the kid is his grandson?"

"Yes," Maddie babbled on, oblivious to the leverage she was giving him. "So you see, my parents are going to be very worried."

"Well, now." Compared to a few moments ago, Frank sounded jovial. "Things are lookin' up, Murray."

"They've got the jacket?"

Jacket?

"You're just trying to find a *jacket?*" Maddie asked. "After all this time?"

"Yeah, a real nice one," Murray said. "It was navy blue. I looked like somebody important in it."

"Double-breasted. Real classy," Frank added.

"I'm sorry." Maddie sounded like she didn't know what to say. "It's probably long gone."

Frank approached. "I'll tell you what. You and junior there are going to stay here while your old man goes through those records and finds out who bought Murray's jacket."

"Don't be ridiculous. *I'll* go through the records for you."

"And while you're doing that the police will come and take us away. Do you think we're stupid, lady?"

Don't answer that.

"I think you're making this unnecessarily complicated. Let's all go back to the center—"

"No."

"Hey—let me go!"

Frank must have grabbed her arm. "Murray, open the door."

"You're going to lock us in a storage shed?"

"That's the plan."

"It's a crappy plan!"

"You've got quite a mouth on you for a preacher's daughter." *Amen*, Steve thought as she was hustled away.

Show time. He opened his eyes, grateful that he was seeing only one of everything—which was more than enough—and shifted his head until he could see Murray working at the door of one of the larger storage units. Frank was holding Maddie. Since she had the baby in her arms, she wasn't putting up much of a struggle, which was good.

She sure was verbally letting them have it, though. Frank pretty much ignored her, but Murray kept glancing over at her, clearly taking her words to heart.

"Will you hurry up with that lock?"

Murray, his orange cap a sick-looking brownish pink in the security lighting, creaked open the door.

Frank gestured Maddie inside with a mocking bow.

Steve decided to wait until the two came back over to the car. He'd go for Frank first.

"How long are you going to keep us in here? It's cold and the baby is going to get hungry soon."

"You're staying until your old man finds the jacket."

"What if he can't?" From the sound of her voice, she didn't think he could.

"You'd better hope he can."

"This is beyond stupid. I'll *buy* you a new jacket," Maddie offered.

"I want that one," Murray said stubbornly.

And Steve wondered why. Had the doubloons been in the pocket? He couldn't think they'd still be there. Or were they sewn in the lining?

Or did Murray just like the jacket and this was all some kind of great, cosmic joke?

"Lock the door and help me with him," Frank said.

"At least give me the diaper bag," Maddie's voice sounded. "It's in the backseat of the car."

"I'll get it," Murray offered. "That's okay with you, isn't it, Frank?"

"Yeah, yeah."

There was the sound of a padlock clicking shut. His cue. Steve braced himself, ready to lunge at Frank's legs.

Maddie was banging on the door. In the background, he could hear the baby crying, the sound echoing off the metal walls.

"What if they don't have the jacket?" Murray was asking as they approached. "Then what do we do?"

"Then we'll find it. It's gotta be somewhere."

"And what if we find it and—"

"Jeez, Murray, don't think about it. You don't have enough brain power."

They were walking side by side. Murray on the inside, Frank on the outside. Closer...closer...

Steve launched himself off the pavement and felt a sharp pain at the base of his skull. Wow. He'd been hit harder than he thought.

"He—"

He connected with a pair of bony knees and found himself back on the pavement, this time cushioned by Frank.

He lifted his fist to deliver a knockout blow—to show Frank how it was done—when he felt himself tilting as a wave of dizziness spread through him.

A second later, he noticed a shadow from behind him and turned in time to see Murray swinging a duck-covered diaper bag.

A diaper bag. Right.

Frank stirred and Steve brought his fist down but never made contact.

The diaper bag crashed into his head packing a surprising wallop.

This time the darkness at the edge of his vision didn't fade, but grew. He'd underestimated Murray, was Steve's last thought, just before he lost consciousness for real.

3

MADDIE FIGURED SHE probably ought to be praying. That's what her parents and sister would be doing right now.

But she wasn't because she'd already prayed more than once—okay, twice—and there wasn't anything new to add. Get her and Luke out of this alive and make sure the gorgeous hunk of a man who'd ridden to her rescue was okay. Same old, same old. She didn't want to make a pest out of herself.

However, if it happened to be a slow night, while Maddie was especially grateful that she'd had a rescuer at all—and the gorgeous part had been a nice touch—it would be really super if all that gorgeousness didn't go to waste. If, say, he'd awaken and, oh, the light in here was really flattering and he turned out to be a decent guy with a thing for preacher's daughters...

Only in her dreams. Maddie was caught in a peculiar no man's land—literally. She wasn't good enough to attract the saintly ones like her brother-in-law, and she wasn't bad enough to attract... well, the ones like this man.

Sighing, Maddie rubbed her arms, then broke down and wrapped herself in one of the blankets in the shed. Touching something that either Frank or

Murray had previously used raised nearly as many goose bumps as the cold did. And in an ironic twist to an already twisted day, she recognized the blankets as the bulk-imperfect fleece ones donated to the center each winter to give out to Houston's homeless the first time the temperatures dipped below freezing. Houston was still waiting for its first freeze, but her parents usually gave the blankets out early anyway.

They gave out hundreds of blankets. And here she was now, with one of them wrapped around her shoulders and another one over the unconscious biker on the floor.

From the piles of clothing, the hot plate, and the mattresses on the floor, Maddie guessed that the two men who'd locked them in here were living in this storage unit. She didn't think people were allowed to do that, but then again, they weren't the sort of men who played by the rules.

There was nothing but the sound of breathing in the shed and for about the fiftieth time, she checked on Luke. She'd spread a receiving blanket from the diaper bag onto one of the mattresses, pushed it against the wall, and built him a little fortress out of old sofa cushions and the diaper bag. He was asleep, but she knew better than to think he would remain so. Gloria had fed him early and had kept him up from his afternoon nap so he would sleep during the rehearsal tonight, which was why he'd been overly tired on the drive from Gloria's to the center, Maddie supposed.

That had only been a little less than two hours ago, but it seemed like forever.

She was becoming impatient....oh, who was she kidding? She was always impatient and the serenity that graced her parents eluded her. Maddie wanted action and she wanted it now, so she was proud of herself for not invoking plagues or anything on Frank, who looked at her funny, and Murray, who just plain looked funny.

There wasn't anything funny about the man on the floor beside her. Beneath the dark stubble on his face, his skin was shaded with gray. From the arguing she'd heard, she gathered that he'd regained consciousness just in time to get hit again.

She'd gone through his pockets, hoping to find a cell phone, but no such luck. She had found his wallet, but had refrained from snooping through it, thinking he'd rouse any moment and get the wrong idea concerning why she wanted to know about him. Except it would be the right idea, which was why she hadn't yet looked through his wallet.

But now, a lot of moments had passed and he hadn't roused.

Once more, Maddie explored the door and gave it a halfhearted yank. Pounding was out unless she wanted to wake Luke, which she definitely didn't. In the uninsulated metal room, his cries sounded a hundred times louder.

The light flickered and Maddie glanced upward. It came from a cheap clip-on lamp attached to a steel support beam. There was only an unenthusiastic sixty-watt bulb, but Maddie knew she was lucky to have any light at all. The cord ran under the door to who-knew-where and she guessed that one of the other unit renters was going to have a larger electricity bill than expected.

Okay, no more pulling on the door. She'd seen the padlock and it wasn't going to be forced open with anything other than a good pair of bolt cutters. She gave a cursory inspection to the debris in the corner, looking for anything she might use as a crowbar to peel the door away from the frame and found nothing, just as she'd found nothing the last two times she'd looked.

Naturally there were no windows—just a couple of screened ventilation openings near the ceiling. They were stuck here until Frank and Murray returned—*if* they returned.

She sighed and sat on the concrete floor beside the motorcycle man. He'd been out too long.

Guilt at involving him nearly overwhelmed her, especially since she hadn't been all that nice to him at the center, but all she could think about at the time was catching up with her car and rescuing Luke.

What would Gloria have done?

Maddie tried to visualize her sister in this position, then realized that Gloria wouldn't *be* in this position. One look at her angelic beauty and the two men would have been stunned into immobility. They certainly never would have pushed her out of the way and stolen her car.

And the man wouldn't have argued about giving her a lift on the back of his motorcycle.

Moaning softly, Maddie dropped her head to her knees. Envious of her sister—how pitiful was that?

It wasn't like Gloria did anything to enhance her looks—she simply said she wouldn't feel right about buying mascara as long as there were hungry people in the world.

So when Maddie needed to buy mascara, she skipped lunch.

Lifting her head, she gazed at the man again. She'd been wearing mascara that day she'd found him shooting hoops in the rec room, not that he would have noticed. She'd watched his gaze skate right over her and knew he'd already seen her sister.

Most men's eyes glazed over after having seen Gloria. Even so, he wasn't the sort of man a part-time kindergarten teacher encountered as she went about the day-to-day business of molding young minds.

He looked dark and dangerous, like a modern-day pirate, and the fact that she was even the slightest bit attracted to him said things about her that she didn't want said.

Tired of thinking of him as a "he," Maddie took his well-worn leather wallet, opened it, and searched for identification.

She noticed immediately that he didn't have a Texas driver's license. Arizona? Did he drive all this way on his motorcycle? She didn't remember if it had Texas plates, or not.

His name was Steven Jackson. Probably went by Steve. That's the way she'd think of him. She did the math and figured out that he was thirty-three years old.

Doug would be thirty-three now, too, she calculated automatically. She couldn't help herself. It had been almost five years since the I-thought-you-knew-I-was-married Doug. He'd been a charmer, and her family would have loved him. With his light, sandy-brown hair, he'd even *looked* like one of them, and so for the first time, Maddie had gone with her heart and ignored her head.

No more.

Maddie was *not* soured on men. She was *not*. But she was cautious.

Perhaps overly cautious since she was related to all the current men in her life except this Steve Jackson, and he was unconscious.

There wasn't much else in his wallet. Maddie saw money, but didn't count it. There was an insurance card, a military ID, a phone card, a platinum American Express credit card, and some sort of flat, credit-card-sized electronic plug-in that looked more impressive than it probably was. Not exactly the wallet of a derelict.

No pictures or stray pieces of paper. No scribbled notes or business cards. Other than the military ID, there was nothing to suggest what he might do for a living.

He worked at something, maybe construction, that required that he use his body, she knew that. He was hard and solid, she remembered from wrapping her arms around him on the motorcycle.

"Well, Steve Jackson. You may have hard muscles, but you've got a soft head. Typical male."

But she'd enjoyed wrapping her arms around a strong hunk of man, even though they were chasing down her car and nephew at the time. She sighed. Who knew when she'd get the opportunity again?

She reached out with her foot and poked his leg. He didn't move.

"Maddie, Maddie," she lectured herself. "Haven't

you learned anything from TV lately? You're supposed to rescue yourself, not sit around and wait for some man to rescue you."

And what kind of shape would this one be in when he woke up, anyway?

She wondered if the two thieves who'd made off with her car would come back. Once they knew where the jacket had gone, they'd probably take off. The stuff here wasn't worth risking arrest for, and while Maddie believed in forgiveness as much as the next person, they must know that as soon as she got out, she'd call the police.

Then she'd forgive them.

Where was the night security for this storage place, anyway? Shouldn't there be hourly patrols, or something? She couldn't believe someone hadn't discovered the light coming from the vent holes and investigated. And Steve's bike had to be around somewhere. Frank and Murray had driven off before they'd had time to do more than push it out of sight.

But she'd heard nothing except a distant metallic clanking and the faraway hum of machinery.

The floor was cold. Maddie reached over and checked Steve's pulse again. The beat was steady, but his skin was cool. In his state, lying on the floor couldn't be good for him.

She wished Frank and Murray had dumped him on a mattress. She'd put Luke on the cleaner of the two, but now she wondered if she could drag Steve onto the second one.

He was a big man, much taller than her father, who was less than six feet tall. Maddie wasn't even certain she should try to move him, but Frank and

Murray already had, so anything she did couldn't cause further injury, right?

All right, then. Maddie got to her feet. There was a lot of floor between Steve and the mattress. She dragged it over next to him, ignoring the musty body odor smell coming from it. She'd smelled worse after a packed night at the shelter.

He was slumped on his side. Maddie spread the blanket she'd used to cover him on the floor and rolled him on it. Her plan was to drag the blanket over the mattress and Steve along with it.

She stepped over the mattress, braced her feet, took the edges of the blanket and pulled. The satin edging ripped right off.

You get what you pay for, she thought and took hold again. Steve was heavy. The blanket was not. Fortunately, it didn't tear. She managed to work both his torso and the blanket onto the mattress, leaving him splayed out on his back like a Christmas turkey.

His head moved from side to side with the motion of the blanket in a way that told her he was still oblivious.

Maddie pulled him onto the mattress as far as she could, then walked around to the other side so she could get his legs off the floor, too.

Legs were heavier than she thought. She tried lifting them one at a time, but her back still complained. And he was perilously close to the edge of the mattress. In fact, once she had one leg on the mattress, there wasn't a whole lot of room for his other one.

Sorry now that she'd ever tried to move him, Maddie sat on the floor and used her feet to push against his hip. He moved, but the mattress did, too.

Well, a couple of inches was a couple of inches. Maddie picked up his black-booted foot and hoisted it toward the mattress.

And countered a totally unexpected resistance from the leg. Already in the process of taking a step, she caught her foot in the hem of her costume and tripped, dropping his leg.

He grunted as it hit the floor.

To her horror, Maddie tumbled toward a chest encased in a tight black T-shirt. She landed right on top of him and bit her tongue. Good grief, his chest was nearly as hard as the floor. Scrambling to push herself away, she felt a heavy weight descend across her back.

"Mornin' already, sweetheart?" he asked, his eyes closed.

"Uh...no. Go back to sleep." She tried to lever herself off him, but his arm held her fast.

"Don't be in such a hurry to leave. Give me a minute to catch up."

Maddie didn't want him catching up to anything. "It's okay. I've, ah, lost the mood."

"Then we'll just have to get you back in the mood." Before she could react, he cupped the back of her head with his hand and brought her mouth down to his in an openmouthed sensual invitation.

Maddie had never been invited to anything like this before. He fit his lips to hers and explored the contours of her mouth, then offered his for her to explore.

It would have been unthinkable to refuse the offer, and since Maddie wasn't thinking a whole lot at that point, everything worked out nicely.

She instinctively mimicked his movements which he rewarded by introducing her to a whole new level of kissing.

His beard scratched her face, and Maddie didn't care.

He'd obviously been eating Mexican food all day, and Maddie didn't care.

He was virtually unknown to her, and Maddie didn't care.

All she cared about was that his searing kiss cauterized the wound that was Doug. It made her forget Doug ever existed.

She now knew one thing with absolute certainty. Doug Fogerty could not kiss. He had pressed his lips to hers, but she would no longer think of it as kissing. The soft gentleness she'd thought was so romantic couldn't even begin to aspire to being a kiss.

This was a kiss. A super-duper, gold-plated, diamond-studded kiss. The kind of kiss that would spoil a women for anything less.

And would make her want more.

She couldn't *believe* she'd mentally beaten herself up for years over getting involved with a married man who kissed like Doug. But she hadn't known any better, had she? And now she did, didn't she?

Which naturally made her wonder what else Doug hadn't done well—and what this man would. His hands started to wander and she knew that if she didn't extricate herself immediately, she was going to find out.

It was a tempting thought, but she had to draw the line somewhere, no matter how crooked.

Wedging her hand between them, she pushed

hard against his chest. He let her go too easily and she shot upward.

"Yeah, time to come up for air." Though his eyes remained closed, his color was better.

Nothing like a little mouth-to-mouth resuscitation, Maddie thought. She'd probably been resuscitated more than he had.

He brought one hand to his temple and rubbed it, a puzzled frown pulling at the edges of his mouth. Exhaling softly he turned his head to the side and was still.

Maddie didn't move, hoping he'd drifted off to sleep. It would also be convenient if he forgot that she'd behaved in a completely inappropriate way. Maddie wasn't sorry she'd kissed him, but she could see how a man would get the wrong impression.

After staring at him for another thirty seconds, Maddie decided that he was probably out again. Slowly, she eased away from him.

He squeezed her bottom.

Maddie yelped and Steve grimaced.

"Did I drink tequila yesterday? Tequila is the only thing that gives me a headache like this."

"No. You got hit in the head. Twice. Move your hand immediately, or you're going for three times."

"You're a feisty one." His other arm wrapped around her. "I like feisty women."

"Keep that up and I'll feist you right into the soprano section of our chapel choir."

He finally opened his eyes. They stared straight into hers. "Mary?" he asked at last.

"Maddie," she corrected through gritted teeth. "My name is Maddie."

"Maddie." Still he stared at her. "Maddie," he said again. "I have one hell of a headache, and you're wearing one hell of a frown. If I owe you an apology for anything, consider yourself apologized to."

Maddie gazed at him disgustedly. "That was the sorriest excuse for an apology I've ever heard."

"If I knew what I was apologizing for, I might be inspired to go into more detail."

"You don't remember anything?"

She watched him arrange his face into a smile, a big, fat fake smile. "I'm sure you were wonderful. Very accomplished."

Maddie's mouth dropped open.

"*Impressively* accomplished," Steve added as though that would help. "But, look, sweetheart, we both had a little too much tequila—"

"*I* didn't drink any tequila. And as far as I know, neither did you, unless you spent the afternoon swilling it at Mama Garcia's."

His eyes narrowed slightly as he obviously tried to remember. "Is that a new strip club? Are you—"

"*No!*" Heedless of where she put her hands, Maddie launched herself off the mattress.

He'd closed his eyes again. "Too bad. That's a great costume in case you ever want to take it up. It's got a sinner/saint thing going that would really appeal to a certain type of guy. Not me, though."

She'd never had a conversation like this with anyone before and found herself horridly fascinated. "Tell me, is there anything about me—anything in my demeanor—that makes you think I'm a stripper?"

"Yeah." He managed a mirthless laugh. "You're with me."

She thought about that for a moment. "So are you only attracted to strippers, or are only strippers attracted to you?"

"Babe, I hurt way too much to have a philosophical discussion with you." He squinted one eye open and looked her up and down. Maddie drew her robes around her ankles.

"So what are you?"

"I'm a kindergarten teacher."

That brought the other eye open. "I'm a little fuzzy on recent history. You mind filling in the gaps for me?"

"Two guys stole my car and you and I chased them. After we caught them, they hit you on the head, then locked us all in here."

Groaning, he rolled onto his back. "Sounds more like they caught us." Without moving any part of his head except his eyes, he looked all around. "Would you mind telling me where 'here' is?"

"Some storage unit by the ship channel. Don't you remember anything?"

HE WAS REMEMBERING more by the minute, including the feel of her pressed against him on the motorcycle and a really great kiss. Unfortunately, he couldn't remember what had led to the kiss, or he'd repeat it, even if she was a kindergarten teacher. The impression he had of her was of a goody-two-shoes kisser who was a fast learner.

Judging by the way she was looking at him and the distance she'd put between them, she'd already learned about him. Smart girl. *He* shouldn't be giving her kissing lessons, the baby's father should.

"How long have I been out?" he asked.

"The first time, or the second?"

Yeah, she'd said something about twice. Steve thought, sifting backwards through recent events until he figured he had nearly the whole picture. Frank and Murray had hijacked her car and she'd insisted on riding behind him because— He jerked upright. "Hey, the baby! What—"

"Shh." She held a finger to her lips and gestured to another mattress.

Steve saw a pastel lump just before the thundering in his head made him close his eyes again. But now that he was sitting up, he was going to do his damnedest to remain so. He pressed the heels of his hands against his temple.

"How's the head?"

"Hurts like hell."

"I'm sorry," she said softly. "And I don't even have any aspirin to offer you. My purse is in the car."

"I'll be okay. Glad you got the kid back."

"So am I."

As long as he didn't move his head, the thundering was just a distant rumble. "Did we decide how long I've been out?"

"It hasn't been quite an hour."

"An *hour?*" He gingerly raised his head. "I got hit with a diaper bag and I'm out for an *hour?* What have you got in that thing?"

"The usual." Maddie rose and retrieved the bag. "Diapers, clothes, sock puppets, a bottle, some formula for emergencies, and this." She held up a book.

A big, thick, children's picture book about Christmas.

Creamed by Christmas. Yeah. Sounded about right for him. "I'm Steve, by the way."

She nodded. "I looked in your wallet because I couldn't stand not knowing who you were. Earlier, I looked for a cell phone—you don't have one, do you?"

He thought of the communications card he carried in the wallet. It wouldn't do any good now. "No."

She sighed. "Then I guess we're stuck here."

Not necessarily. "The last thing I remember is tackling the short guy and getting hit by the tall one. Fill me in on what happened after that."

She mostly told him stuff he already knew, but he let her talk because then he wouldn't have to be concerned with remembering what she knew and what she didn't know about Frank and Murray.

"They've gone to find a jacket?" This was the part he was interested in anyway.

"Yes. They think Murray's grandmother gave it to our thrift shop. The thing is, we would have sold it or given it away long ago. The only way we would still have it is if we put it in our interview collection."

"What's that?"

"We keep back the good-looking suits and outfits to lend to people who're job hunting. If the jacket is as good as Murray says it is, then maybe we do still have it."

Slowly and carefully, Steve got to his feet. He stood still until his head quit pounding. "Do you remember the jacket?"

"Are you kidding? Why would I remember anything about a jacket I supposedly saw a year ago?"

He looked down at her. "Murray seems to think it was really something—something worth ransoming people for. Was it a designer label? I'll bet you don't get a lot of those. Did it have unusual ornamentation? Maybe he left something in the pockets." Steve tossed off the last.

"We go through the pockets," she said, answering his unspoken question. "If we find anything obviously valuable, like jewelry, we attempt to contact the previous owner. That doesn't happen very often."

Steve began a perimeter check. Just how locked in were they? "You keep records of your donors?"

She sighed heavily. "I do, and it's a royal pain."

Steve found himself smiling. Not exactly the properly grateful sentiment someone in her position should express. Yeah, well, a little ingratitude just made a person more interesting.

He glanced back at her and she wore the look of someone who regretted her words. He wanted to tell her it was more honest to say what she felt rather than fake something she didn't, but it wasn't his place.

"Thieves were parking stolen merchandise with us and then breaking in and stealing it back," she continued, "so I made sure we started keeping records. If Murray can remember when his grandmother made her donation, maybe there's a chance we can trace his jacket."

Steve had continued walking around the room. It was mostly empty, except for Frank and Murray's stuff. He pushed on the walls. They gave, but not much. He stepped back and looked at the ceiling. He could climb to the vent holes, but wouldn't be able to fit through. Maddie was swathed in layers of burlap, so all he had to go on was the feel of her, but he didn't think she could fit through the openings, either.

He reached the door and stared at the knob.

"There's a padlock on the outside," Maddie told him. "If you're going to try to break through, be careful of the lamp. It's bad enough being locked in here without it being totally dark."

"I'll keep that in mind." Steve squatted down to examine the fittings and the hinges. The door was built to keep people from breaking in, not people breaking out. The bolts holding the hasp could be removed by a determined man with the right tools.

Or by a determined man.

He walked back over to Maddie and spoke in a low voice. "You say you've got food for the baby?"

"A full bottle and about eight ounces of formula. That's not much." She looked over at the quiet lump. "I just hope he sleeps until we get out."

The baby food gave them some leeway.

Steve considered his options. They were safe for the time being. He didn't know where his bike was and even if it were still outside and operable, it would be hard to transport a woman and a baby. He could probably figure out a way if he had to, but he'd rather not. He'd also rather not leave them alone here.

Ideally, Frank and Murray would return with the jacket and Steve would—barring anyone being armed with a diaper bag—persuade them to tell him if it had any connection to the missing doubloons.

He decided to hang around here with Maddie. If the center had Murray's jacket, they'd most certainly give it to them since Maddie and the kid were being held for ransom.

There was always the possibility that Frank and Murray would just take off and leave them in the shed, but Steve didn't think so. They weren't hardcore criminals—just two petty crooks who'd apparently stumbled onto the biggest haul of their life and never knew it.

Yeah, he'd stay with Maddie. If Frank and Murray couldn't shake the jacket out of the center, then Steve would try tracing it himself. In the meantime, he'd stay put.

4

SECRETLY, MADDIE HOPED Steve would kick down the door. He looked like a kick-the-door-down type of man. But when he rose to his feet and continued his walk around the room, she swallowed her disappointment.

She was ready for a kick-the-door-down sort of man in her life, she realized guiltily. Her father and brother-in-law were so gentle and kind and *good*, that Maddie exhausted herself trying to be gentle and kind and good whenever she was around them.

It shouldn't take so much effort, she told herself. But it did.

There were times when she thought they were too good—in fact, she could visualize her father inviting Frank and Murray to have dinner before they came back and released her.

Well, maybe not. But it could happen.

Steve was poking through the clothes and things that Frank and Murray had mounded against the walls of the shed. He wouldn't find anything useful, she knew, but let him look for himself.

He completed his circuit and, giving the baby a wide berth, returned to where Maddie sat on the edge of the mattress. As she watched him walk across the floor with a much surer gait than when he'd first stood, it struck her that she'd put aside a lot of her natural caution since they'd met, and even then, hitching a ride on the back of his motorcycle barely counted as an introduction.

She'd assumed a lot about him—that he was an altruistic man for instance—on very little. When Maddie had asked her about him after that day in the rec room, Mama Garcia had said he hadn't caused any trouble and was a good tipper. And then he'd helped Maddie get her nephew back.

And she'd kissed him without a qualm.

But other than the sparse information she'd gleaned from his wallet, she didn't know him at all. She was becoming as trusting as her family.

Looming over her as he was, he seemed much larger than when he was unconscious. She'd known about the muscles, too, but they seemed larger and stronger when in use.

She and this man were alone together, Luke notwithstanding.

Wincing slightly, he sat next to her on the mattress, not too close, but not at the other end, either. By all rights, Maddie should be feeling nervous, but she didn't. Praying that her instincts hadn't failed her, she asked, "Figure any way to get us out?"

After cautiously exploring the back of his head with his fingers, he propped his elbows on his knees and exhaled. "I've got a few theories. Right now, as long as the kid is asleep, I think we're better off waiting for those two punks to return."

Maddie didn't want to wait. She wanted him to put those theories into action right now. "How long do we wait?"

"Until you feed the kid the last bottle."

This wasn't the gung-ho escape Maddie had hoped for. "Are you sure?"

"Ask yourself what you'd do if we got out now."

"Go back to the center. They're going to be worried." When he didn't react, she went on a little fishing expedition, "Isn't someone going to be worried about you?"

"No."

He answered unhesitatingly and without elaborating so Maddie didn't know if he was just traveling alone, or was *alone* alone.

"And how do you plan to make it all the way back to the center?" he asked. "Walk?"

He knew she couldn't walk. They were miles from East Street. They were in a totally industrial area, no grocery stores, houses, gas stations or telephones. "Are you telling me you wouldn't give me a ride?" Maybe he wasn't such a good guy after all.

He gestured to the other mattress. "You *and* the baby?"

"Oh." Maddie involuntarily glanced over at her nephew.

Steve gave her a puzzled look and Maddie guessed she seemed like an uncaring aunt, but she wasn't used to having babies with her. She hadn't forgotten Luke—she'd forgotten she'd have to deal with him. Usually she went over to Gloria's or babysat at the center.

"I don't even know if my bike's still out there. Do you?"

"I think it must be because they drove off right after they dumped you in here. I've been listening in case anyone came by, and I haven't heard anything."

"That's encouraging news. About the bike."

For him, maybe. "I hope I get my car back."

He almost smiled. "Why?"

Was he serious? "Because it's my car! Maybe where you come from it's different, but here in Houston, if you don't have a car, you're stuck."

He looked unimpressed. "It needs engine work or you're going to get stuck anyway."

Maddie sat a little straighter. "I am aware of that." She was never *unaware* of that. Each time she turned the key in the ignition was an act of faith.

"Then why don't you get it fixed?"

Because people's charitable donations seldom include free car repair. "I'm still paying off the new tires."

"Yeah, I would have gone for those first, too." He caught her eyes, his expression verging on approval.

It was a tiny, little *crumb* of emotion and Maddie felt herself gobble it up. Good grief. How pathetic was that? "I had to get new tires," she felt compelled to confess. Mustn't get approval under false pretenses. "Otherwise, the car wouldn't pass inspection."

He gave a world-weary chuckle. "Isn't that the way life is sometimes? We've got to be forced to do the stuff that's good for us."

"You're right!" Maddie twisted around on the mattress. "That's the way *I* feel—like I have to be *forced* to do the right thing."

He was staring off into space and at first, Maddie thought he was going to ignore her, then he slowly turned his head and looked at her consideringly.

"But you always end up doing the right thing, don't you?"

She nodded.

"Well, Maddie that's the difference between us. I don't." There was a challenge in his gaze before he looked away, as though he thought she was going to recoil from him.

Hardly. "I don't *like* doing the right thing all the time—does that count?"

A slow smile spread across his face and he laughed softly, but didn't answer her. Maddie decided to take that as a "yes."

"Now, about your car—since your husband doesn't appear to be mechanically inclined, you could contact an auto repair school and let the students have a look. They couldn't hurt it," he added under his breath.

"Oh." She'd never thought of that. "What a good idea. I know of a place, too." The idea of having a smooth-running car and a checking account balance off life support made her smile. "Thanks."

He'd been sitting in profile, occasionally glancing over at her. Now, for some reason, his glance stuck, then dropped to her mouth. Was he remembering their kiss? *She* was.

"And..." She swallowed. "I'm not married."

"That doesn't surprise me."

Maddie wasn't sure of the reaction she'd expected, or even why she'd bothered to correct him, but she sure didn't expect to be insulted. "Why?"

His eyes moved up and down in a brief, but telling, sweep over her costume and the Christmas book she still held on her lap.

The nerve of him. Maddie's grip tightened on the book. "Just because I don't look like one of your tacky stripper girlfriends doesn't mean I couldn't be married. There are plenty of men who prefer subtlety and decency to...to obvious and—and..." She quickly gestured in the area of her chest.

He gave her an unrepentant look. "They're lying if they told you so."

And she'd enjoyed *his* approval? "Don't judge all men by your low standards."

"I try not to judge them at all, but when I do, my standards are flexible according to the occasion."

"As are your morals?" Maddie had experienced quite enough moral flexibility.

"Who said I had any morals?"

Maddie started to retort in kind, but stopped when she remembered Steve yelling from across the street at Frank not to hit her. That was moral outrage, for sure, and he deserved credit. "I do," she said instead. "I say you have morals."

The smart-alecky grin he'd been wearing vanished. He not only looked surprised at her, he looked shaken. He turned his head away for several seconds and appeared to stare at the door. "I have my own morals," he said at last. "They might not agree with yours or anybody else's, but I don't give a damn."

Maddie thought about the cuss can in the center foyer. Men who swore and cursed were obliged to put a coin in it for each infraction of the center's no-swearing-rule.

There were nights when Maddie surreptitiously made change for a nickel. There was also the night when a gloriously drunk Raymond Barlevorn shoved a ten-dollar bill into the can, then let loose with a string of curse words that turned the air blue.

Her father turned Raymond out of the center. He also gave him the ten dollars back and told him to use it at the eight-dollar-a-night flophouse two blocks over. Maddie would have kept the money, just as she'd kept Steve's ten dollars that day.

She knew he'd have done the same thing.

They weren't as different as he seemed to think.

He continued talking. "When I said I wasn't surprised that you weren't married, I only meant that you don't seem like a woman who has a man in her life just now."

That was either a veiled apology, or a veiled reference to the way she'd kissed him. Well, so what? "On the other hand, you seem like a man who has a lot of women in his."

"Never for very long, sweetheart. Never for very long."

"You're the love-'em-and-leave-'em type?"

He gave her a half smile. "They're the ones who want to be left and I'm happy to oblige."

"What a sad way to go through life."

"How's that?"

"All alone."

"Only if you don't like your own company."

Maddie thought about that. "What if you don't?"

He looked at her, studying her in the dim light. "Seems to me if that's the case, then it isn't fair to inflict yourself on someone else."

"So if you like yourself, then you would want to be with someone."

Steve leaned back on his elbows. "Maddie, we're

going to get along a whole lot better if you don't preach at me."

"I wasn't preaching, was I?"

"You were coming real close."

She exhaled. "Thanks."

"Thanks?"

"My parents would be happy to hear it."

"They feel you've strayed too far off the straight and narrow path?"

"They've never said, but they didn't have to." She'd never told them Doug was married. All they knew was that she'd been crazy in love and then one day, she was back living at the center, refusing to talk about dropping out of grad school after only a summer session.

They'd never met Doug. They'd wanted to, and Maddie had been eager for him to meet them. Now, she was glad they hadn't.

"Hey."

She looked up at him.

He held her gaze for a moment and Maddie thought he had nice brown eyes—nice once the hardness had left them. The kind of eyes that had seen a lot. Sad eyes with a touch of compassion in them. "Everybody makes mistakes."

Could he read her mind?

"You've got to stop feeling guilty. Learn the lesson, forgive yourself, and move on."

Steve was a man of unexpected depths. In fact, Maddie had never realized how shallow Doug had been until just this moment and it shook her a little. "Now who's preaching?"

He glanced toward the ceiling. "Shouldn't a lightning bolt strike right about now?"

Maddie laughed softly. "Not you. You're a good man."

"No." The whole tone of his voice roughened. "I'm not. Remember that."

He was wrong. "But you helped me."

"I didn't do anything I didn't want to do."

"You let me ride behind you when you didn't want to," she pointed out.

"Except that. And even if I'd had a helmet, I shouldn't have."

"Why not?"

In answer, he gestured around them.

Maddie couldn't have him blaming himself for their predicament. "I'd rather be here with Luke than back at the center without him."

"Personally, I'd rather be in a nice warm bed with—" He stopped and slid a glance toward her. "A TV remote."

She grinned. "That wasn't what you were going to say."

"But that's what I said."

Maddie was disappointed. She was used to people cleaning up their speech or behaving differently when they found out who her family was. That's why she'd enjoyed college so much. No one knew her. No one expected her to be a saint because she'd come from a family of saints.

She'd felt free.

And guilty because of it.

And she felt guilty now because while everyone

must be worried out of their minds about her and Luke, she was secretly enjoying talking to Steve.

Obviously, he was the sort of man who'd never bother with her under ordinary circumstances, and truthfully, she'd probably never approach him. But since they were stuck here together, well, she found him...okay, she'd admit it. She found him intriguing. Attractively intriguing.

But would he fit in with her life? No.

Would she fit in with his? From what she knew of it, no.

Did she like her life as it was now?

Oops. Maddie swallowed. She hadn't meant to think about that.

She studied him.

He didn't have any tattoos. Or at least no visible ones. She thought all men of his sort had tattoos.

He probably thought all women of her sort were nice, gentle, goody-goodies. Well, she wasn't. Maddie's gaze fell to the picture on the cover of the book in her lap. Since Gloria had copied the costume for the Christmas pageant, Maddie looked like the book cover come to life. She slipped the book back into the diaper bag, then looked over to see if he'd noticed.

"What are you looking at?"

Caught. "You. Your head. When we get out, come back with me to the center. We have a clinic."

"I'll be fine."

"I'd feel better about everything if someone looked at your head."

"I said I'll be fine."

He probably would, but Maddie didn't like the idea of not seeing him any more. "You know...we can find a bed for you at the center, too. It won't have a…TV remote, though."

"I've got a hotel room," he said dryly.

"Are you headed somewhere for Christmas?"

"No."

He didn't like her prying. But she wasn't prying. She was making conversation. "The center always has a huge community turkey din—"

"No."

Grouch. But he was entitled, she reminded herself. "Mama Garcia will be there so her café won't be open."

"She doesn't mind the competition from the soup kitchen?"

Maddie shook her head. "We never serve Mexican food and we don't stay open all day long."

There was silence as Maddie tried to think where she could lead the conversation. She wanted to find out more about him. For some reason, she *needed* to find out more about him.

But Steve wasn't looking at her—he seemed to be gazing at Luke—and she could see the back of his head. It wasn't a pretty sight and she felt another prickle of guilt.

He was still looking at Luke when he said without warning, "Tell me about your big mistake."

She was surprised he cared. "He was married."

Steve raised his eyebrows and turned to look at her. "I didn't figure you for the type."

"I didn't know," she felt compelled to say. "Not until he went back to his wife."

"Jerk."

"I didn't know that either."

He laughed a low, rusty chuckle. "At least you haven't lost your sense of humor."

Maddie felt warmed by the approval in his gaze.

"Do you ever see him?" Steve asked.

"No. He was a visiting professor my last year of college. Because of him, I decided to stay on after graduation and go to grad school." Steve still looked interested, so Maddie continued, "It was a wonderful summer which I thought was just the first of many summers, but when his six months were up, he went back to his wife and child. And I dropped out of grad school and came home."

There was no censure in his gaze and Maddie found it a relief to unburden herself without hearing a lecture in return.

"Did your parents give you a hard time?"

That had been the lecture she'd been avoiding. Maddie stared at the hem of her costume. "They didn't have to."

THE LOOK ON HER face pretty much said it all—along with the little souvenir asleep on the mattress over there.

Steve was struggling to stamp out the wholly unwanted feelings of protectiveness for Maddie that were penetrating the armor he wore around his emotions.

He didn't want to feel anything for her. He was never going to see her again. Feeling anything was a waste of energy and it wasn't like him, either.

It must be the hits he'd taken to his head.

Or all the talking. She talked a lot. Other women

he'd been with had talked a lot, too, but they didn't have anything to say.

And they usually didn't expect him to talk back.

He was having an actual conversation here. When was the last time he'd talked to a woman he wasn't either interrogating or planning to sleep with?

He couldn't remember.

"So how about yours?" she asked.

"Mmm?"

"Your mistake."

"Who says I made one?" Automatic defense.

"You sound sadder but wiser and you only get that way from experience." She pulled her legs under her as though settling in for a long chat. "So spill it."

He was amused in spite of himself. "Which one of my many mistakes should I spill?"

Maddie made a dismissive gesture. "The big one, of course. It'll be the most interesting."

And the one most likely to put a damper on the conversation. Well, maybe he wanted her to stop yapping. "I got married."

She blinked, her expression wary. "Are you still married?"

"Nope."

Her face relaxed. "There's your mistake then."

"You're wrong," he said, shaking his head. "The divorce was the best thing I ever did."

"What happened?"

"We both signed some papers and—"

"That's not what I mean and you know it."

He did know it.

"What went wrong with your marriage?"

Man, she was nosy. "Maybe I don't feel like talking about it."

She lifted a shoulder. "Then don't. I was just making conversation."

He waited because he knew her curiosity would win eventually. But she didn't even look at him as she sat on the edge of the mattress and pulled threads out of the hem of her costume, making the fringe longer.

She worked slowly, drawing out the job. After she removed a thread, she stretched it out beside the others she'd collected on her side of the mattress, making sure the ends were all even. Then she'd pick at another thread and pull it.

The little rasping sound was getting on his nerves.

"I wasn't the kind of man she should have been married to, okay?" Why did he feel like he had to say anything to her?

Maddie continued fraying without looking up. "What kind of man *should* she have married?"

"A better man than I was." He could feel words never said welling up inside him. "It wasn't her fault. None of it."

"What did you do?"

Failed. Failed miserably at the kind of life he'd thought he'd always wanted. "I tried to be somebody I wasn't."

"Who did you try to be?"

She was good. She had just the right note of detached interest in her voice. Sort of a tell-me-if-you-want, no-big-deal-if-you-don't tone. It worked for him. It worked big time. "I tried to be a good husband—or what I thought a good husband was. I bought a house in a nice neighborhood, I went to work, I came home in time for dinner. I took her out to eat or to a movie once a week and I even went to church on Sundays."

"When did you shoot pool and knock back a few beers with the guys?"

"I never did that!" And he was damn proud of it.

She finally looked up from raveling her hem. "You seem like the sort of man who'd enjoy an evening out with his friends."

"Yeah, so?"

"Didn't you miss it? Didn't you miss them?"

"I was married."

"Marriage isn't supposed to be a prison."

A chill went through him. *I feel like I'm in prison!* he'd shouted at poor Celia. "When you're married, you have obligations and responsibilities." He'd tried to be everything his father hadn't been and in the end he was afraid he'd become just like him.

"True, but what about fun? What about love?"

Steve almost shivered. "What about them?"

Maddie didn't say anything. She liked to talk, so why wasn't she talking now? But she just looked at him, which meant he had to think about what had just been said. He didn't like to think.

Long ago, as part of his training for Special Forces, he'd been subjected to interrogation techniques that might be expected if he were to become a prisoner of war. None of them was a barrel of laughs, but the one he'd hated the most was the bright light shining at him, just like in old black and white movies. He'd felt so exposed, as though everything in him was laid open for anyone to see.

He felt that way now. With a few pointed questions, Maddie had exposed junk he'd thought he'd buried. How did she do that? How did she know?

Fun. Love.

He didn't know how to have fun—the right kind of fun.

Love? What was that? He'd grown close to his buddies as they'd survived mission after mission. Any one of them would have taken a bullet for the others.

Was that love?

Celia had been so sweet, so delicately pretty. She'd seemed like an exquisite flower that had taken root and bloomed in the ugliness of his heart. She'd been so trusting and so pure. So perfect.

He was a better man when he was with her. Secretly, he'd thought that if a person like Celia loved him, than he must not be so bad after all.

He'd tried to be the husband she deserved. He was proud to be seen with her, proud of the house she kept. He wanted to protect her from all the ugliness he knew was in the world. From all the ugliness that had been in *his* world.

Was that love?

If so, it wasn't enough.

Maddie leaned forward and he felt the coolness of her hand touch his. Softly, she tapped his knuckles. He looked down and with surprise saw both his hands clenched into fists.

Beneath her hand, he consciously uncurled his fingers. She tucked her fingers around his and squeezed gently.

Steve stared at her hand covering his then slowly

raised his eyes to meet hers. In her blue gaze, he saw compassion without pity and sympathy without censure.

She understood. Probably more than he realized, and probably because of what she'd gone through, herself.

It didn't matter how. What mattered was that he'd needed to be understood, though he'd never admitted it to anyone. Apparently she'd figured that out, too.

Their hands warmed and Steve felt warmer inside, too, as though his emotions were defrosting. Which was a romantically mushy image and not like him at all.

A second later, just before he became uncomfortable, she withdrew her hand. "So. Tell me about her."

This woman was persistent. Steve knew all he had to do was refuse to answer, but somehow, he couldn't. Gazing into the distance he summoned the image of his wife as she'd been the day he'd proposed to her. "Celia was like a beautiful, fragile flower, as innocent as—" He heard a noise and looked over at Maddie.

She was making gagging motions with her finger. *"What?"*

"Oh, please. No woman wants to be treated like a 'delicate flower as innocent as a newborn lamb,' or some such garbage."

He stared at her. What had happened to compassion? What about her sympathy? And women said they wanted men to open up and "share" their feelings more. So he did and look what happened.

She grimaced. "Oh, now I've hurt your feelings. I'm sorry."

"You haven't hurt my feelings. I don't have any to hurt."

Her finger started for her mouth, but she saw the expression on his face and obviously thought better of a repeat performance. "Having feelings isn't a sign of weakness, you know."

"Actually, I don't know. Emotions get in the way of clear thinking."

She appeared to give his words some thought.

Maddie in thought made him uneasy. The thing about talking with her was that he never knew what was coming out of her mouth next. Just when he thought he knew where the conversation was headed, she gave it a twist.

"Do you really think emotions cloud your thinking?"

"I *know* they do."

"How?"

She looked genuinely interested and Steve found himself telling her stories about his stint in the military. He told her how training was supposed to take the place of fear and explained how they were cautioned not to become too attached to members of the team. He'd come to think of the men as the brothers he'd never had, anyway.

And regretted it when his bunkmate hadn't made a rendezvous on time and Steve had endangered the whole team by waiting for him.

Maddie's eyes were wide with concern. "Did he make it?"

"Yeah."

She relaxed. "Then it was a good thing you waited."

"No. We were late and didn't beat the guard change at the border." He wasn't going to tell her which border, but she seemed to know enough not to ask. "They knew something was up and our whole unit had to activate twelve hours before we were supposed to."

His sentimental delay had been stupid and the whole team had been split up and reassigned after that. The guy had never even thanked him.

Maddie tilted her head to one side. "Did your new team work as well as the old?"

It hadn't.

"Did it?"

"No," he admitted reluctantly, knowing what she was going to say next for once.

"It didn't work as well because you didn't have an emotional bond with your teammates."

"Maybe," he acknowledged.

"Definitely." She seemed very sure of herself. "Anyway, I'm glad you weren't just an average guy when you came riding to my rescue. I guess I was lucky you were sitting on Mama Garcia's patio."

Maddie's beaming smile made Steve uncomfortable.

Luck had nothing to do with him being there. If he hadn't been sitting on Mama Garcia's patio, then Maddie and her kid wouldn't be here now. He'd prefer not to tell her that, yet. In spite of Murray recognizing him, Steve didn't think the two knew who he was and the less Maddie knew, the less she could blab.

"I also feel better about waiting here. This must be nothing to you."

He touched the lump on his head. "Getting conked on the head isn't exactly nothing and it's never part of my plan."

She made a sympathetic face and hugged her knees. "Tell me more stories."

And so he told Maddie things he'd never told Celia. Celia had never asked. No woman had.

But Maddie...Maddie was different. He supposed he'd known that right from the start. Her education was like Swiss cheese—full of holes. From working at her parents' shelter, she'd seen a lot of life, but seeing it was different than experiencing it, and Maddie didn't have as much experience as she thought she had.

Specifically in one particular area. He hated the thought of her giving herself to the married creep—especially since the guy obviously hadn't been any great shakes in the sack, judging by Maddie's untutored kiss.

Which prompted a whole line of thinking he knew he should avoid. Steve, without being falsely modest, knew he was good in the sack. Actually, he could provide references attesting to his being considerably better than good. He caught himself watching Maddie and half wanting to show her a few moves. Then a few more, then—

"You feel better now, don't you?" They'd been talking for who knew how long. Or, to be fair, Steve had done most of the talking and Maddie had listened.

He did feel better. So help him, he did. He scowled.

She laughed. "You don't want to feel better, do you? You've been wearing your hair shirt for years. I'll bet you enjoy feeling guilty. In fact, you're using your guilt as an excuse to avoid relationships. It fills up your heart. Take the guilt away and there's room for love."

"What are you? Some kind of psychic flimflam artist?"

She looked incredibly self-satisfied. "I must be right or you wouldn't be calling me names."

He wasn't going to talk to her anymore. He wasn't. She saw too much.

"Now you're pouting."

"I—do—not—pout." He stood—to stretch his legs, he told himself. Not to get away from her.

When he looked back down at her, he caught her stifling a yawn. "Go ahead and sleep."

"That's okay. I've just been sitting in one place for too long."

She started to stand up but Steve reached down and touched her shoulder. "Maddie—sleep. I'll catch first watch."

She smiled and he realized what he'd said.

"Okay, but only because it won't be for long. Luke is bound to wake up pretty soon." She took the lumpier items out of the diaper bag, put it under her head, and curled up on the mattress.

Steve moved away and stood by the door. No new sounds stirred the night.

He checked his watch. It was just past nine-thirty—plenty long enough for Frank and Murray to have terrorized the Givens into searching what records they might have.

Face it. Frank and Murray took the car and headed south for the border.

All along, Steve thought he'd had them pegged as minor lawbreakers. Two dumb guys who'd caught a bad break. He hadn't figured them for the type of men who'd leave a woman and a baby locked up without food or water.

Unfortunately, it looked like that was exactly what they'd done.

5

MADDIE DIDN'T THINK she'd be able to sleep. It wasn't all that late and though talking with Steve helped pass the time, she still expected Frank and Murray back any moment. She wanted to be alert and ready to grab Luke and...and do whatever Steve told them to do. He was obviously an expert in these situations.

Besides, sleeping while he paced the room made her nervous.

She rearranged the soft contents of the diaper bag until it was an almost comfortable pillow and the baby lotion scent counteracted the mattress smell. She *should* probably try to relax.

If she thought there was any chance that Steve would continue to open up to her, she'd keep talking. He'd led a fascinating life, but it was easy to see that he carried a deep sadness within him. He'd convinced himself that he was a loner, but Maddie thought he didn't want to be.

Well, it didn't matter. In a few hours he'd ride that big, black motorcycle out of her life and never give her another thought.

She had a feeling he'd be lingering in *her* thoughts for far longer.

MADDIE, THE PREACHER'S daughter, was one dangerous woman.

Steve sat with his back propped against the door and watched her sleep from across the room. He...liked her. Genuinely liked. And so help him, he thought he might be more than a little attracted to her. Why, he had no idea. He liked women with good bodies. Usually, he saw the body first, then was attracted. He knew what he was getting.

But both times he'd seen Maddie, she'd been wrapped in so many layers of baggy clothes, he didn't even know if she had a body.

So what was he attracted to?

She had a good voice, he thought. It was a comforting voice. He could imagine her in front of a room full of little kids, using calm, comforting tones to direct their day.

She was also pretty, he decided. It was sneak-up-on-you prettiness. He'd never pick her out of a lineup of showgirls, but would he pick a showgirl out of a lineup of teachers?

He wasn't going to pick her at all, though. Even if he were interested, she came with too much baggage. With his background and the way he'd messed up his marriage to Celia, Steve wasn't about to screw up a kid's life.

Maddie's breathing changed to the even tenor that told Steve she was asleep. She was too trusting. She was in luck this time, because he was going to live up to that trust.

Steve leaned his head against the metal wall, which hurt, so he rested his forehead on his knees. Here he was again, alone with his thoughts.

THE NOISE SOUNDED like a cat. Steve jerked his head up, checked his watch and found that he'd dozed for ten minutes or so.

Getting rusty, old man. He was awake now though and the mewling sound that had awakened him came again.

Pressing his ear to the door opening, he listened, then saw the pale lump on the other mattress move.

The baby—what had she called him? Luke. Luke was awake.

He glanced at Maddie, but her breathing didn't change.

Luke was making little distressed noises which became more and more insistent until they gathered into a cry. Steve saw the baby's head bobbing. Good man. If food didn't come his way, he went looking for it himself.

"Maddie," he called softly.

No response.

Luke now cried in earnest—wailing cries that demanded action from anyone within earshot.

Steve, a man of action, stood, intending get the baby and carry him over to Maddie.

He squatted next to the mattress. "Hey, there, little guy."

The little guy didn't hear him.

Steve had zero baby experience. In fact, his entire body of infant knowledge was gleaned from television, the movies, and diaper commercials.

Okay. Crying and food. He knew about that connection. As carefully as though he were handling an armed bomb, Steve picked up the baby, still wrapped in a pale blue blanket, instinctively supporting his head when it fell back.

The baby quieted. Steve held him at arm's length out in front of his body and stared at him. He was a solid little chunk of a human. Good set of lungs he acknowledged when Luke, sensing the person holding him needed reminding that he was hungry, started crying again.

"The man wants food, so we'll get him some food."

Steve saw the bottle over by the still-sleeping Maddie. He held Luke to his shoulder, but figured his leather jacket wasn't the most baby-friendly material, and set Luke back on the mattress as he shrugged out of the jacket.

Luke howled so loudly that his lower lip quivered. He wasn't too thrilled about being caught up in the blanket, either. His feet kicked and his hands bunched into fists.

"Okay, okay." Steve couldn't believe Maddie hadn't come leaping off the mattress. Even he was affected by the power of that cry.

Cradling the baby in one arm against his chest, Steve was nonplussed when Luke opened his mouth and went on a food search. "Hey, little guy, I don't have the right equipment." In fact, even the thought of the biological use of the right equipment was wrecking several great memories.

Steve offered Luke the knuckle of his index finger and was surprised at the force with which the baby clamped down.

Luke figured out he'd been had by the time Steve made it over to Maddie. Incredibly, she still slept. It was the equivalent of sleeping through an air-raid siren. The emotional upheavals of the evening must have caught up with her, so Steve decided to let her sleep.

The bottle was in a thermal tube that he zipped open in a maneuver that would have been easier if he'd had three hands. It took him a minute to figure out the mechanics of the bottle, cap and nipple assembly.

Luke reminded him that time was a wasting.

"Hang on, fella." As soon as he could, Steve pushed the nipple toward Luke. The baby met it halfway and began gulping frantically.

Gulping too quickly as it turned out. He choked, sending adrenaline spurting through Steve's body. As soon as Luke finished coughing, he started crying for the bottle again.

This time, Steve propped his head at an angle and things worked better. Within moments, the baby had settled into a rhythm and he relaxed.

He felt a coolness on his skin and realized he'd been sweating as much as he ever had on a clandestine mission. But Luke didn't seem to care that this was Steve's first time to give a baby a bottle. Steve couldn't remember when, or if, he'd even held a baby before.

They were so little, but so powerful. And incredibly single-minded.

After a few good swallows, Luke opened his eyes and fixed a dark-blue stare on Steve. *Who are you?* it seemed to ask.

"Feeling better now?"

The baby didn't blink.

"Hey, you can pull back on the eating. I'm not going to take it away."

A trickle of milk ran out of the corner of Luke's mouth. Steve wiped it off with the blanket and in doing so, his finger touched the baby's cheek.

The skin was astonishingly soft. Celia had had soft skin, but nothing like this. Steve brushed his finger back and forth on the baby's cheek and Luke turned his head to that side.

Steve stood there for a long time, staring at the baby and slowly shifting his weight from foot to foot. Occasionally, he'd stroke his finger across the top of the baby's blond, fuzz-covered head, marveling at the feel. He found the soft triangle at the top of the baby's head and detected his pulse through it.

He felt...he didn't know what he felt. This was just a baby. He'd never thought about babies—or at least he hadn't since he'd divorced. And truthfully, not all that much while he was married. He'd always assumed he and Celia would have kids because that's what people did, but he hadn't thought about what caring for a baby would be like. Maybe he'd thought Celia would handle everything. Celia would have wanted to.

He tried to imagine his own father holding him like this and couldn't. His father hadn't had a nurturing cell in his body.

His father hadn't had a sober cell in his body.

"But you're not going to have that problem, are you kid? You've got your whole life in front of you and it's going to be a good one. You've got a great mother and yeah, it's a tough break to grow up without a dad, but growing up with no dad is better than growing up with a drunk one."

Steve tilted the bottle up a little more as Luke continued to drink from it. One of the baby's hands slid off the side of the bottle and encountered Steve's fingers, grabbing tightly onto one.

"You've got quite a grip there, kid. Yes, you do." Steve waved the tiny fist back and forth. "Yeees, you *do.*"

He was talking baby talk. Involuntarily, Steve looked around to see if anyone had overheard. Of course, no one was around but Maddie, and she was asleep, but it had been a close call.

If he was going to be talking to the baby, then he ought to be giving him advice—man-to-man information that his jerk of a father should have been around to give. Who knew what babies planted in their subconscious until they could understand it?

"Okay, kid, listen up. I've got a few pieces of advice for you. Buy low, sell high, never stiff a waiter and change your oil every three thousand miles. Remember that it's fast cars and loose women, not loose cars and fast women, and never pay sticker price for either."

Luke actually stopped attacking the bottle when Steve spoke. "Hey, you are listening. Okay, let's talk about women. You don't hit them. Ever. And don't go giving your mom any lip, either. You do, and you answer to me. Tell her you love her and be a man— say it like you mean it. I know, she's going to get on your nerves 'cause she tends to get preachy, but she's a good woman and being stuck with good folk won't be so bad. You won't ever have to see your mom get a cracked rib to give you enough time to run outside and hide from your dad. I used to have to wait under the porch until my old man passed out and I could sneak back inside."

Steve was silent for a moment. "He found me one time and then passed out beside the hole in the trellis. I couldn't get out and had to spend the whole night under the porch."

He'd been in worse spots since then, but he couldn't remember being more afraid. But Luke didn't need to hear about that. "It was the best hiding place while it lasted and anyway, we moved right after that and our new house didn't have a porch."

Looking down at Luke, he said, "I don't know why I'm telling you all this. It must be because you're such a great listener."

In response, the baby's head turned just enough to let the bottle nipple fall out of his mouth. He'd fallen asleep.

Steve smiled. "Boring you, am I? Yeah, sometimes I bore myself."

Now what? He hadn't changed the baby's diaper and wasn't he supposed to burp a baby after it ate? Gingerly, he shifted Luke's position until his warm body was draped over his shoulder. Almost immediately, there was a burp that would have come in about third place in any bar belching contest in the country.

"Way to go, bud."

Slowly, tempted to skip the next part, Steve set Luke back on the mattress. Now, diapers. He looked across the room where Maddie was using them for a pillow. Well, too bad.

Steve quietly approached her and knelt down. The

trick was to extract a diaper without awakening her. Shouldn't be any harder than stealing the key to the liquor cabinet from beneath the supply sergeant's pillow.

He reached for the opening of the diaper bag and stopped, noticing moisture at the edges of her eyes.

Damn it, she'd been crying before she fell asleep.

A piece of her hair had fallen over her eyes and Steve gently moved it back toward her cheek. In doing so, his finger brushed against her skin, much as his finger had brushed against the baby's cheek. Not as soft as he expected, which actually was like Maddie, herself. She was tough when she needed to be and soft when it counted.

He'd never met a woman who could be both before.

"I'm going to get you out of this, Maddie," he breathed and reached for the diaper bag opening. The bag's snaps weren't fastened, so all he had to do was ease his hand inside and pull out a diaper. Slipping his hand under the weight of Maddie's head, he felt soft plastic and pulled, barely moving her.

Haven't lost the touch, he thought and headed back toward Luke.

MADDIE OPENED HER eyes and watched him walk across the room. He thought the baby was hers, she realized. At some point, she'd have to correct his assumption, but that could wait.

She'd been eavesdropping on Steve's conversation with the baby for a while now, and, though she supposed it was wrong of her, she wouldn't have missed one syllable. And she didn't want to miss the diaper changing, either.

"Hey, you're awake," Steve murmured and knelt on the floor beside Luke. "Now, how do we get into this thing, huh? You've got about a million snaps here."

A freshly fed baby was at his most appealing, Maddie knew. Luke moved his arms and kicked his legs and made cute baby gurgles which Steve responded to with a few nonsense words and tickling his tummy before taping the diaper in place.

He stood. "Okay, let me find some place to stash this and I'll come back and tell you the best way to negotiate a car deal."

He wrapped the dirty diaper in something he found among Frank and Murray's trash, and then sat on the mattress and picked up Luke, who was blowing bubbles. It was his new trick and soon he and Steve were both blowing them.

Maddie swallowed as she felt the tears well up again. Steve had cradled the baby against his broad chest and had no idea how appealing he looked at the moment, or that he had a straight line right into her heart.

He'd obviously had a rotten childhood, but no matter what he thought or how he acted, he was basically a good and decent man.

A girl could do a lot worse. A lot. Maddie knew, because she had.

He was talking to the baby—something about counter offers—and his low rumble of a voice had quieted her nephew.

As Maddie listened, the rumbles vibrated against

her heart. Even knowing that the circumstances they were in artificially heightened emotions didn't matter. She wanted to be cradled against that chest of his. She wanted his strong arms to hold her. She wanted to feel Steve's gentle touch again and again.

Why was she always attracted to men who weren't available?

She forgot she was pretending to be asleep and sighed out loud.

Steve looked in her direction, so Maddie continued the charade by stretching and sitting up.

"Hey, look, Mommy's finally awake." Steve turned a sleepy Luke to face her.

Maddie held her finger to her lips and tiptoed across the room congratulating herself that she didn't immediately fling herself at him. He, after all, held her nephew in his arms, but Maddie knew that if they were quiet, Luke would go back to sleep for another few hours before he woke up for keeps.

She smoothed out the blanket on the mattress, and motioned for Steve to put the baby back in his nest. After moving Luke's favorite terry-cloth elephant within reach, she motioned for Steve to follow her across the room.

"I thought mothers had this built-in baby radar, or something," he said. "But you slept right through all the crying."

"I'm sure my sister, Gloria, does. You remember Gloria—you probably saw her working at the thrift shop? Blond? Angelically pretty?"

He nodded.

Maddie thought he'd remember. "Luke's her son. My nephew."

His face turned to stone and he stared hard at her before speaking. "That's not your kid?"

Maddie shook her head, a little confused by his stern reaction. He didn't think she lied to him, did he?

"The married guy—?"

"Thank goodness, no." She shuddered. "That was over four years ago in August."

His eyebrows knit together. "I thought—"

"I can see how you would," she interrupted. "But I didn't mean to give you that impression."

He glanced over at Luke, then back at her.

Was he disappointed?

"Gloria's got the flu. I'm just taking her place in the pageant for the dress rehearsal," Maddie explained. "Are you...you aren't mad at me, are you? I didn't mean—"

"No, no. It was my mistake." As he spoke, he was looking about the room, clearly preoccupied with something else. "I didn't realize the kid wasn't with his mother. She must be out of her mind with worry."

"If anyone has told her, then yes. I imagine she is. John, too. My brother-in-law—he's Luke's father."

"We've got to get out of here," Steve said abruptly.

"But what about everything you said? What about—"

He was already striding across the room. Maddie hurried after him.

"I'll go for help and send somebody back for you two," he said, examining the door.

"Now, wait a minute. What about everything you said before? What about waiting?"

"The plan has changed."

Steve quickly went over to Frank and Murray's stuff.

Maddie trailed behind. "Don't I have a say in the plan?"

"No." His tone told her not to argue.

"What if those two guys come back here while you're gone?" That was a question, not an argument, she told herself.

"Then that means they've come back to let you go." He glanced at her before pawing through Frank and Murray's eating utensils. "They'll probably keep the car, though."

"That's okay. I know how to negotiate for a new one, now."

Steve stopped and gave her a grin, then did something totally unexpected.

Stepping over the pile of debris, he came right up to Maddie, put his hands on either side of her face and kissed her. "You're something else, you know that?"

Maddie didn't move so she'd be in the right position in case he wanted to kiss her again.

Steve looked into her eyes and rubbed a thumb across her cheek.

Maddie thought moving *closer* might be okay. She stood on tiptoe and wound her arms around his neck.

"Maddie..." he warned.

He moved his hands to her arms and Maddie knew he was going to pull them away.

So she kissed him.

He tugged halfheartedly, then crushed her to him as he gave her the kiss of her dreams.

Surrounded by his strong arms, pressed against his chest, Maddie found it easy to live in her dream world—a world where there was a future with Steve. A world where his kiss expressed more emotion than technique.

Maddie put her heart into her kiss. So what if he didn't want it?

He murmured her name in a way that thrilled her, even though she knew he was only caught up in the moment. It was a great moment—several moments even—and she was caught up in them, too.

He kissed her jawline and the sensitive area beneath her ear. She smiled at the prickling of his beard.

He broke the kiss once to study her. "You're going to regret this."

"I would regret *not* doing this."

"I'm not the person you think I am. Don't make me into some kind of hero."

"Okay. Besides, you'd look funny in a cape."

That prompted a small smile. "Maddie, you've got to understand that after we get out of here, we nev—"

"I know, I know!" she said impatiently. "But I'm trying to forget. Why you insist on reminding me when you could be taking advantage of me in my weakened state, I *don't* know."

He pressed his forehead to hers and chuckled softly, then proceded to take advantage of her in her weakened state.

And Maddie found she could be very weak, indeed. Weak enough to chance giving little Luke a cousin. Except that the weaker Maddie got, the stronger Steve got.

She made little pulling motions toward the mattress, awful as it was, and he planted his feet right there by the door and wouldn't budge.

"Hey, pay attention," he murmured.

"Huh?" was her sensuous response.

"I'm kissing you. Concentrate on that."

"Kissing can be good."

"Kissing can be *very* good."

Kissing could be terrific.

He drew back until he was barely touching her lips, then traced around the outside of her mouth with the tip of his tongue, giving all her nerves a wake-up call.

He followed that with a series of tiny, nipping kisses that made Maddie clutch him and try pressing closer, even though she couldn't get much closer.

A little whimpering sound escaped her and Steve drew back.

Her next whimper was louder. "More."

"Maddie, Maddie." Amusement sounded deep in his throat. "You deserve better than me."

"There's no one better than you."

"Sure there is." He brushed her hair off her forehead and brushed his lips there. "I'm not a white-picket-fence kind of guy."

"I'll teach you." She sounded desperate and knew it. "You taught me kissing—I'll domesticate you."

He shook his head, his eyes sad. "I don't want to learn."

Maddie knew that. She'd hoped otherwise, but could accept him on his terms. Just as long as there were terms at all.

For so long she'd tried to do the right thing in her life—now she was trying equally hard to do the wrong thing with the wrong guy.

And it felt right.

"Okay, you've done the obligatory noble speech, so now you may round the corner and slide into second base." She tightened her arms around him and closed her eyes.

"You're giving me a walk when I want to hit one out of the park." He nibbled her lips apart and touched her tongue with his.

And that would be okay, too. Shivers raced through Maddie and she felt both hot and cold at the same time. Steve deepened the kiss until Maddie wasn't sure where she began and he ended.

And she liked it that way.

She matched his every movement until she felt confident enough to try a few of her own, all designed to get closer to him.

Just as she felt that she was going to be turned inside out, a car door slammed.

Before she had time to realize that she was no longer in Steve's arms, he'd shoved her behind him.

Shuffling sounded outside the storage shed.

"Hurry up, you moron!"

There was a clink. "I—I dropped the key!"

"Where?"

"By your foot."

More shuffling, then a thud.

"Ow!"

"Gimme that!"

A louder metallic scraping, then the chink of the padlock releasing. Seconds later, Frank and Murray barreled through the door and slammed it behind them.

Steve started forward. "What—"

"Shh!" they shushed in unison.

Giving them a wary look, he positioned himself off to one side.

Luke started to cry.

"Keep the kid quiet!"

Maddie looked at Steve and he nodded imperceptibly, so she quickly went over to Luke. Frank snatched Murray's cap off his head and wrapped his hand in it, then unscrewed the light bulb. The room plunged into darkness.

In a few moments, Maddie's eyes adjusted to the pinkish glow coming through the vent holes and she sat on Luke's mattress. Picking him up, she gently rocked him back and forth until he stopped crying.

"You hear anything, Frank?" Murray carefully folded up the edge of his knit cap and positioned it on his head. It wasn't the same bright orange one that had clashed with his hair, but a dark one with green lettering that said Ski Colorado.

"Not with you yammering, I don't."

"Suppose you two tell—"

"*Shut up!*" Frank spoke in an urgent whisper and pressed his ear to the door.

Steve stopped talking and did the same.

Murray looked like he was about to cry.

Something had obviously frightened the two men

and Maddie was glad Steve was smart enough to try figure it out instead of arguing with them.

After several minutes of listening, Frank nodded to himself.

"Okay, everybody remain calm." Frank sounded like he was trying to convince himself more than anything. "You—" He pointed to Maddie. "Get the kid's stuff. And you—" He pointed to Steve. "I want you to arrest us."

6

STEVE KNEW THERE had to be a trick. "I can't arrest
you."

"Sure you can." Frank held out both fisted hands,
then nudged Murray into doing likewise.

"Yeah," Murray said. "We know our rights and
we have the right to be arrested."

"I don't carry cuffs," Steve told them. "I'm not a
policeman."

"Bounty hunter then? Whatever. We surrender,"
Frank said. "Take us in."

"You guys jump bail?"

"Maybe not so recent, but hey, check it out you
could get lucky." He gestured toward his hands.
"C'mon. Let's move it."

"Tell me what's going on."

"That's what I'd like to know," Maddie said with
an accusing look at Steve.

"Don't get confused about who the bad guys are
here," he cautioned her.

"Well, maybe I'm not sure anymore. Who are
you?"

"Not now. All you have to know is that I'm good."
He gestured to Frank and Murray. "And they're
bad."

They stared at each other and he did his level best

to look good. He thought about smiling, but didn't think it would help. She was just going to have to make up her mind to trust him.

She narrowed her eyes. "You told me you weren't good."

"That was different."

"Are you going to arrest us, or not?" Frank asked.

"Not. I can't," he said, still looking at Maddie.

"Well, *I* can," she said. "Citizen's arrest. Tie them up, Steve. Here. I've got a rope belt on my costume."

"You don't have to tie me up," Murray said. "I'll keep my hands on my head." He laced his fingers together and did so.

"Jeez, keep your arms down, Murr. We gotta breathe."

"Then I'll sit on my hands." He folded himself up on the floor.

Steve turned his attention to Frank. "I've got a first-class headache that you two are responsible for and I'm not in a real good mood. So start talking."

"Okay, here's the deal." Frank dropped his hands. "Me and Murray, we was tipped off to a little job. Easy pickings. Some big deal wedding and all we had to do was take the master key card and go shopping from room to room while everybody's downstairs."

An inside job. Steve had always thought so, though investigators insisted that all the hotel personnel had passed a lie detector test. "Who gave you the master?"

"We don't know."

Steve walked closer to Frank, backing the smaller man up until he was pressed against the metal wall.

"My head hurts, so maybe I'm not thinking too clearly. But I'm thinking clearly enough not to buy that story."

"But that's what happened!" Murray burst out. "We picked up an envelope—"

"Where?"

"At the front desk in the hotel. I wanted to, but I didn't have good enough clothes and it was a fancy place. Frank did, so he got to. That's why I took the jacket, so next time, I could do the high-class stuff. I'm tired of being the one who has to hide in the Dumpster."

If Steve's head hadn't hurt before, it would now.

"Moron," Frank said, but without heat.

"Let me make sure I understand—some unknown and inexplicably generous benefactor just *gave* you the hotel master key," Steve said sarcastically.

"Not just *gave*," Frank said. "Right off the bat, we were supposed to get a book out of some suite."

Finally some progress. "What book?"

"*A Christmas Carol* by Charles Dickens," Murray recited.

That caught him off guard.

"Why? Was it a first edition?" Maddie asked from across the room.

Steve supposed it was too much to hope that she'd remain quiet.

"Lady, I don't know and I don't care. We were just supposed to take the book and put it in another room, see? After that, whatever we wanted to do with the key was our business."

As far as Steve remembered, a copy of *A Christmas Carol*, valuable or otherwise, hadn't appeared on the list of insurance claims or property stolen in the case. "So after you took the book you went 'shopping' from room to room?"

"Yeah."

"And while you were 'shopping,' did you take some gold coins?"

Frank clasped both hands to his head. "You cops never let up, do you? We told you we don't have any gold coins and you go on and on about it. They offered us early parole. We woulda said something."

Steve narrowed his eyes. "I don't know...you had a light sentence and those gold coins were Spanish doubloons. Find the right buyer and you'd be set for life."

"I want to know what's scaring them now," Maddie said. "If they're scared, then I'm scared, too."

"She's a smart lady." Frank pointed for emphasis. "You ought to listen to her."

"Some guys are after us," Murray said.

"What guys?" Steve had an exclusive on the recovery. Only someone very inexperienced and very foolish would try to horn in on his territory—and that included both police detectives and feds.

"Bad guys," Murray said.

Instead of calling him a moron, Frank nodded, which gave Steve a sinking feeling. "What happened?"

"We went back to the center, see, and her old man made us wait in line."

"Didn't you tell him why you were there?"

"Yeah. He said we should wait in line."

Steve gave Maddie a startled look.

"He has to keep strict order, or people would mob the place," Maddie explained.

The guy's daughter had been kidnapped and he wanted to finish ladling out free food first. Steve shook his head. Maddie's father didn't sound much better than his.

"While we was waiting, Murray gets to talking with this fella—"

"He was my new friend," Murray said. "We traded caps."

Steve glanced to the dark one now on Murray's head and remembered how easy the bright orange one had been to spot. He guessed what happened next and Frank confirmed it.

"A little while later these two dudes hustle this guy away and he don't come back." Frank glanced at Maddie, and lowered his voice, "And it's gettin' kinda noisy from the side alley, if you know what I mean."

Steve knew.

"He was my friend," Murray said. "So I had to help him."

"Yeah, Murray, I know." Frank rubbed his face wearily. "The guys, they were asking him about a jacket—"

"The same jacket you two are looking for?" Maddie interrupted.

Steve gestured for her to keep quiet. Frank and Murray were finally talking and he didn't want to stop the stream of information.

"Who knows? But the poor schmuck, he didn't know what they were talking about, so Murray yells, 'Leave him alone, *I* got the jacket.'"

"He was my friend," Murray repeated. "I wanted them to stop hitting him."

"And they came after you then?" Steve prompted.

"Sure." Frank shrugged. "We figured they'd chase us for a little while, then give up."

"We could run faster because they had on Sunday shoes," Murray said.

"Sunday shoes?" Steve looked at Frank.

"Leather with smooth soles. They were snappy dressers. Latino."

Something tickled Steve's memory. While he was trying to think what it was, Maddie was talking to Frank and Murray.

"You think they're still chasing you?" she asked. "All the way here?"

Murray nodded vigorously as Frank spoke. "We hid in the food line outside the shelter. The guys ran right past us and we think we're home free. Then they came back and we heard them talking on their phone. I'm telling you, they knew our names and they were reportin' to somebody." Frank's voice grew more urgent. "And that's the God's honest truth. Now take us in."

"Good idea," Maddie agreed. "Take them in."

"I'm not a policeman," Steve repeated quietly.

"An FBI agent?"

The hopeful look in her eyes faded when he shook his head. "Then how do you know so much about them?"

"I was hired by the insurance company—"

"You're an *insurance* agent?" She looked at him incredulously.

"Not...." He started to explain, then thought better of it. "Yes. I'm an insurance agent."

She rolled her eyes. "Oh, brother."

"I was hired to find the gold doubloons these guys stole."

"We didn't steal any doubloons!" they protested.

"But you stole my car and kidnapped a baby." Maddie clutched the sleeping Luke closer to her. "If the big, bad insurance agent won't drive you to the police station, then *I* will."

"Wait." They could do as Maddie suggested, but Steve was closer to finding the doubloons than anyone had been and sending Frank and Murray back to jail didn't suit his purpose right now. "We'll take them back to the center and keep an eye on them there."

Maddie looked at him incredulously. "After what they've done? Are you nuts?"

Maybe, but Steve was counting on Maddie's father to keep Frank and Murray in line. They seemed to respond to his authority.

"Don't want to go to the shelter." Murray shook his head. "Don't want to go. And I want my jacket."

"Forget the jacket!" Frank yelled, then immediately swore and listened at the door.

"I don't want to! It's the only one I ever had that fit! I got these long arms, see?" He held them out. "And jackets are always too—"

"Long arms?" Maddie interrupted sharply.

Startled, Murray jerked his in and crossed them over his chest.

Luke began crying in loud, deep-breathed wails.

"What about long arms?" Steve asked her.

Maddie shook her head as she tried to sooth her nephew without success. "Nothing."

Something, but he'd let it pass for now. Long arms... Steve sucked in his breath. "The Gorilla." He raised his voice over the baby's crying. "You took the Gorilla's jacket."

Murray looked wounded.

"Don't you call him names!" Frank stepped forward belligerently.

"I'm not. Does the name Enrique Cortavilla—aka Cortavilla the Gorilla mean anything to you?"

"Nah." Frank shook his head and Murray, after looking at Frank first, did as well.

"Think," Steve prompted.

"Like a person could think with that noise!"

Maddie wasn't having any luck with Luke. Poor kid. Steve walked over to the mattress and held out his arms for the baby.

Maddie hesitated, then surrendered the crying infant.

Steve smiled reassuringly at her as he took the baby, but even with the dim light, he could see her face had gone pale. "Hang on a little while longer, okay?"

"But—"

"It'll be okay."

She clamped her lips together and gave a tight nod.

Steve put Luke over his shoulder and rubbed his back as he walked slowly toward Frank and Murray. "We'll get you back to your mommy soon," he murmured, and as before, it seemed the vibrations of his voice soothed the baby.

How about that? He wasn't bad at this. He looked over at Maddie who managed a weak smile.

Women. They want men to help, but don't trust them when they do.

He settled Luke more firmly against him. It was the first time he'd confronted perps while holding a baby. Didn't do much for his tough image. Maybe he'd switch to reasonable. "So, about Cortavilla—"

"Look, we never heard of the guy," Frank interrupted. He'd responded better to tough.

Ignoring Frank, Steve concentrated on Murray. "He has long arms—that's why he's called 'The Gorilla'—and he was a guest at the wedding. Not somebody you'd want to cross and it looks like he's figured out that you took his jacket. Do you remember the room where you stole it?" They'd been in a lot of rooms, so Steve wasn't expecting much.

"The first one with the book," Murray mumbled.

Well, well, well. So the book in Cortavilla's room had been the original target—and according to reports, Cortavilla had never reported a book or jacket stolen. Just the doubloons. "Did you take anything else out of that room?"

They shook their heads. "I kinda got the idea we weren't supposed to," Frank admitted.

They weren't lying. It would have been easier if they had been. Now that meant the doubloons had been hidden either in the book or the jacket. Logic pointed toward a hollow-core book—except the men hunting Frank and Murray had wanted the jacket.

Steve exhaled. Well, he was never called in for the easy recoveries, was he?

Luke was a warm, moist lump against his shoulder. Steve held his hand against the baby's head, idly brushing his fingers over the silky hair. Now what?

He was deciding how much to tell Frank and Murray without alarming Maddie when she marched up to Frank and held out her hand. *"Give me my car keys."*

"And leave us here? No way."

"I need to get to my sister's right now. *Give me the keys."*

Oh, great. She was already alarmed. "Maddie, we'll—"

She whirled on him. "You don't understand—I know where their stupid jacket is. My brother-in-law has long arms, too, and when the jacket came in, he tried it on and it fit, so he's got it now."

"Be quiet, Maddie." Steve didn't shout because he didn't want to wake Luke. He probably should have.

"I will not be quiet. I'm going to their house, getting the jacket and flinging it out onto the street so the Gorilla people can find it and take it away."

"Maddie, calm down." She was about to blow everything.

"Calm? There are men beating up people over that jacket. *These* two stole my car, locked me up, and you want me to be calm?"

"Yes. Now we'll all go back to the shelter, then I'll go get the jacket from your brother-in-law."

An engine coughed with sickening familiarity.

Maddie's eyes shifted, then widened. "They're gone!"

While Maddie had been ranting, Frank and Murray had slunk away. Steve swallowed the first word that came to mind so he didn't blister the baby's ear. He got to the door in time to see Frank drive off.

If he'd been seconds sooner...if he hadn't been talking to Maddie...if he hadn't been holding a baby...

"Grab your stuff and come on."

"Why? What are we doing?"

"Giving Luke his first bike ride."

THIS WAS ONE time Steve wouldn't have minded being stopped by the police so they could take Maddie and the baby off his hands. They were seriously cramping his style.

He found his bike shoved out of sight in the alley between the rows of storage sheds. Luke was presently heavily padded and roped inside the bike luggage pack like a papoose. Consequently, Steve drove as though he was carrying an open aquarium.

He was violating safety laws right and left, but he had no choice. Frank and Murray had a head start, but Steve thought he had time to take Maddie and the baby to her home before they figured out where her sister lived.

It's a good thing Frank and Murray had left when they did. A few more minutes and Maddie might have drawn them a map. Now, they'd probably go to the center and ask where Maddie's sister lived. Knowing the parents, they'd probably tell them.

Maddie was a lot more quiet and subdued than the Maddie he'd known the past few hours. Good. He didn't want to argue, or explain what he was doing. He just wanted to do his job and collect his recovery fee.

They'd been riding about fifteen minutes before Steve had cooled down enough to stop being angry with her. Bottling up his anger had never been good for him. He needed to let it out, and then he was over it. The problem was that letting it out usually involved a lot of yelling on his part.

Maddie would probably just yell back and he'd get angrier.

He knew he wasn't mad any more when he became aware of how tightly she held him. He'd liked the way her arms felt around his waist before, but now that he knew she wasn't married, he was allowed to enjoy it.

He'd been enjoying an awful lot where she was concerned. He should probably feel guilty about kissing her. She was a girl looking for the big *C*— commitment—and he was into the big *T*—temporary. *T*'s shouldn't mix with *C*'s, no matter how kissable they were, because no matter how many times a guy waved his *T* flag, a *C* thought he just hadn't found the right woman yet.

Steve had already found the right woman and hadn't known how to be the right man.

Maddie's life would drive him nuts. Those parents of hers would expect their son-in-law to work at the shelter. They'd certainly expect a setup pretty much like the one he'd had with Celia.

And that wasn't the way Steve wanted to spend his life. He just wanted to do his job and stay out of everyone's way.

There he was, thinking again. He half hoped Maddie would start talking again so he *couldn't* think.

But Maddie said nothing for the next forty-five

minutes and then only when Steve asked her where she lived.

"At the center, why?"

He slowed the bike and pulled into the parking lot of an all-night convenience store. Turning until he could see her face, he asked, "You *live* at the shelter? All the time?"

She nodded. "My family has an apartment there."

"Is that where your sister lives?"

"No, their house is about ten minutes away from the shelter—unless you're trying to drive to it in traffic. But there isn't much traffic this time of night."

"Be grateful for that."

"It's a beautiful old house," Maddie went on, her self-imposed sentence of silence apparently commuted to time served. "When they moved in, the neighborhood wasn't all that great, but people are buying up property and renovating it or building new. Gloria says they couldn't afford to buy into the area now. She and John are keeping the house until they get an offer big enough to pay for their kids' education. I think that's smart..."

Realizing nerves were making her talk, Steve let her babble while he figured out what to do next. He hadn't anticipated that she lived at the shelter. He couldn't take her and the baby there, not with Cortavilla's men around. Frank and Murray were more bumbling than dangerous, but that had been before they'd been threatened. Now they were scared and that made them unpredictable. Unpredictability equaled danger in Steve's book. That meant taking Maddie and the baby to her sister's was out.

So where was he going to take them?

"As long as we're stopped here, do you have thirty-five cents I can borrow to call them?" Maddie asked.

"What are you going to tell them?"

"Well, duh!"

To her, a phone call was a reasonable request. He drew a deep breath. "Maddie, just tell them you and Luke are okay. You can't say anything about the jacket, or Frank and Murray or anybody else. And... no police."

She gazed at him with an incredulous expression on her face. "Why not?"

"Can you trust me?" he whispered, then leaned down and lightly kissed her parted lips.

She didn't move, but when he pulled back, she sighed. "That is *so* not fair."

He grinned and dug thirty-five cents out of his pocket. As Maddie got off the bike and walked over to the pay phones, Steve scanned the area for low-lifes, then looked back at Luke, asleep and oblivious to everything, thank God.

Steve wondered if they made baby motorcycle carriers. Probably, although it would be difficult to beat the hard luggage shell the baby was in now.

"They weren't home and there wasn't an answer at the center, either. I didn't leave a message," Maddie volunteered as she climbed back on the bike and handed him his change. "We'll get there in half an hour, anyway."

Steve hesitated.

"Hey—let's go," she urged him.

"Okay." Slowly accelerating, Steve left the parking lot and melted back onto the street. At the next intersection, he headed west instead of east.

Maddie didn't say anything until the buildings started getting fancier. "The easiest way to get to my sister's house is to stay on Travis and take it out of downtown."

Steve talked back over his shoulder. "I'll get directions from you later."

He saw Travis as he went past.

Maddie did, too. When he didn't turn, she poked his shoulder. "You missed the street."

He shook his head.

"Yes—it was back there!"

"We're not going to your sister's house."

"Then where are we going?" she shouted.

He hesitated, knowing he was in for an argument. "My hotel."

7

"YOUR *HOTEL*? I don't want to go to your hotel!"

He didn't answer, but he didn't have to. He was driving.

If it hadn't been for Luke, Maddie would have jumped off the motorcycle the next time it stopped at a red light. Instead, she held herself as far away from Steve as possible and fumed. She couldn't believe he was going to dump her and the baby at some cheap hotel somewhere.

No matter what, she wouldn't stay there. Somewhere, there had to be a phone and Maddie's first call was going to be to the police.

Trust me. And she thought her parents were gullible. She should have already called the police. And she shouldn't have given him back his thirty-five cents.

The scenery had improved while she'd been fuming. They were in the heart of the high-rent theater district where the office buildings were clean and shiny and had glass in all their windows, and the restaurants served pastries on the actual day they were baked.

And Steve was slowing. Not only was he slowing, he was slowing by the Lancaster Hotel.

The Lancaster was one of those places Maddie

knew about but had never been in. Small, elegant, and luxurious, it epitomized everything that was not in her life and she secretly wished was.

She knew she shouldn't want wasteful luxury, yet she did. Even now her heart beat faster just being close to it.

Steve turned onto the front drive, drove right up to the beveled glass and brass doors, and stopped by the doorman.

The doorman touched the brim of his hat. "Good evening, sir."

To her everlasting shame, Maddie's heart pounded. Surely *this* wasn't Steve's hotel.

Steve turned off the motor. "How's it going, Woody?"

"It's been a quiet evening."

"I think I can liven it up for you."

"I have no doubt, sir."

Steve motioned for Maddie to get off the bike.

Through the magnificent portals lay temptation. To be tempted by such shallowness was Maddie's secret shame. She shook her head and stayed put.

Steve's expression didn't change. "The clock's ticking. The faster you get off, the sooner I make it over to your sister's place."

"Take me with you."

"You and the baby will be safer here."

Steve was right and arguing with him was wasting time. Maddie climbed off the bike onto her wobbly legs only because she intended to find a phone and call the police as soon as she could.

Not because temptation had won.

At her sudden capitulation, Steve gave her a suspicious look. "Woody, would you keep an eye on the bike while I get these two settled?"

"Certainly, sir."

Luke roused as they were extricating him and Maddie could tell that this time, it was going to take another bottle before he went back to sleep. Even then, it might take a while. She stared inside the enticing lobby. Maybe even days and days. She didn't know. She'd only rarely fed Luke a bottle, and never this late at night before. Gloria was still nursing him and all Maddie had left were two of the tiny bottles of emergency formula in the diaper bag.

With an insistent hand in the small of her back, Steve propelled an awestruck Maddie toward the hotel's front desk.

The place screamed—but quietly and elegantly—luxury. This was in direct contrast to Luke who was just screaming.

Maddie propped him over her shoulder as she'd seen Steve do earlier and it seemed to comfort the baby somewhat. But Maddie knew it was only temporary.

An ornately decorated Christmas tree dominated the cozy homelike lobby. How many holiday dinners could have been delivered for what the tree and ornaments had cost? The thought surprised her. She was thinking like her parents. This was a good thing, she told herself.

"You must be a heck of an insurance agent," she said to Steve.

"I'm the best at what I do, so I can afford to indulge myself when I want to." He spoke matter-of-factly, without a hint of boasting.

Maddie was impressed in spite of herself. She was also unwillingly attracted by the confidently casual way he took charge.

After greeting the concierge, Steve gestured to Maddie and the whimpering baby. "I'm going to leave these two in your safe keeping. Go ahead and put them in my room. We'll also need a crib, diapers, and baby formula—Ms. Givens can give you the details."

"Very good, sir." The concierge was on the phone almost before Steve finished speaking.

He reached for a pen and pad of paper, an elegant pen and creamy paper, Maddie couldn't help noticing, then turned to her. "Tell me where your sister lives."

Luke was fussing again. Maddie shifted him to her other shoulder before answering.

"Maddie?" Steve prompted.

"I'm going to tell you. Gee, it's so rare that a man actually *asks* for directions I was savoring the novelty."

He didn't smile.

She told him how to get to her sister's house, watching as he scribbled down the address.

He ripped off the paper, tossed the pen back onto the marble-topped counter, and stuffed the address into his jacket pocket. "You'll be fine here. Ask the concierge for anything you need."

The temptation was strong within her, but she knew what she had to do. For now, she nodded and smiled. "'Bye."

Steve narrowed his eyes, then took her arm and

led her away from the desk. "Promise me you won't call the police."

"Okay." She'd just have the concierge do it.

"I'll let your family know where you are and they can come and get you two when it's safe."

Take your time a little voice whispered.

Maddie was going to have to get out of here before the little voice was the only one she could hear. "Great. Sounds like a plan."

After another sharp look, he nodded a goodbye, then strode toward the glass doors. Halfway there, he pivoted and came back to where Maddie still stood swaying from side to side with Luke.

"What?" she asked innocently.

"You can't call the police."

"That's what you told me."

"But I didn't tell you why. Here's what's going to happen. I'm going to get the jacket, make sure Frank, Murray, and the Cortavilla men know it and draw them away from your family. *Then* we bring in the police."

"You're going to be the bait." That was unnecessarily noble, if you asked her.

"Right. Because if the police come, Maddie, everybody will run and just wait until the cops leave. Even if by some miracle the cops catch everyone, Cortavilla will send more men. Trust me, you don't want that."

He was throwing around the "trust" word again.

He made everything sound so logical. But was it truly logical, or did she just want to believe so she could spend some time wallowing in decadence and drooling over a room-service menu?

Tough call.

She caught him looking at her, and smiled widely. "Good luck."

He stared at her, then paced in a circle and swore under his breath. The rarefied atmosphere of the Lancaster lobby quivered.

"Luke's hungry, so I need to feed him now." Maddie started backing away.

Steve came to a halt and scowled. "Hand me the kid."

He'd surprised her, but Maddie gave him Luke, frankly glad for a respite.

Steve held the baby against his shoulder and murmured something Maddie couldn't hear. She heard what he said next, though.

"Frank and Murray are a couple of goofballs. Enrique Cortavilla is part of the Mexican Mafia."

Maddie gasped.

"They're pros, Maddie. They don't leave witnesses."

Luke had quieted, lulled by Steve's voice. Maddie was glad the baby couldn't understand the words. She wished *she* couldn't understand the words. They sure put luxury in perspective.

"Frank and Murray are in way over their heads and don't have any idea. Sending police officers into a situation like that without warning means people get hurt," Steve continued. "They'll be more effective if they have the option of alerting their special teams."

"You're scaring me." Her family was in danger and she was lusting after room service. Maddie was ashamed.

"Good! I want you scared. I want you too scared to leave my room." He handed her back a now-quiet Luke.

"Are *you* in over your head?"

"Not me." He gave her a quick smile. "I've got to go."

"But..." *But what if I never see you again?* Well, she couldn't say *that*, but she sure thought it. "Be careful."

"That's my middle name."

Maddie watched him stride off, and once more, he pivoted and came back to where she stood. "I...have to do this."

Holding her face, he kissed her hard and fast. "'Bye squirt," he said to Luke and this time, when he strode off, he made it all the way through the glass doors.

BY STEVE'S COUNT, he'd kissed Maddie on four separate occasions. This was not good. Or rather, the kissing was good, but he was sending her signs that a reasonable woman would interpret as interest on his part.

Since he wasn't prepared to act on that interest, it would be better for everybody if he didn't broadcast it.

When the job was over, he'd move on. That was his life and he liked it that way.

He took a corner and missed Maddie's weight behind him. He also missed wondering what she was going to say next. He missed arguing with her.

He missed kissing her.

In his whole life, Steve didn't think he'd ever

missed a woman when they weren't together—not even his wife.

But he missed Maddie, and he'd left her just a half hour ago.

It was obvious that Cortavilla's men weren't the only danger to him tonight.

He found Maddie's sister's house without any trouble. It was in an older neighborhood with big yards and mature live oaks that cast huge shadows from the moon and the streetlights. Discreet white Christmas lights made the shadows blacker. Perfect for concealing people up to no good. Or motorcycles.

In spite of what he'd told Maddie, Steve half expected to see a police car parked by the curb. The house lights were on, which told him people were awake.

After circling the block and not seeing anything suspicious, he cut the engine on his bike and pulled it into the driveway hoping anyone not familiar with the house would assume that the classic Harley belonged there.

Even though he'd thought a lot about Maddie on the drive over to her sister's place, he'd also considered how he wanted to approach the people inside. His goal was to gain their trust and to see the jacket, then figure out what they should do next.

Steve climbed the two wooden porch steps, and rapped on the door. He'd already reached into his breast pocket for his wallet to show them his identification when the door opened.

Caught off guard, Steve froze.

A slight, bearded man with sandy hair stood on

the other side of the screen door. The man didn't appear to be armed.

"Yes?"

People shouldn't throw open doors in the middle of the night. He outweighed the man by fifty pounds at least and all that stood between them was a flimsy screen door.

These people wouldn't last thirty seconds with Cortavilla's men.

"Hi, I'm Steve Jackson." He finished taking out his wallet, and opened it to both his military ID and the insurance company's card.

The man glanced at it, but didn't ask to take the card so he could call and verify Steve's identity. After hesitating, Steve put it away. "I've got news about Maddie and your son. They're fine—"

"Praise the Lord," the man said, and opened the door. "Come in and tell us." He actually reached out and took Steve's arm. "My name is John, and that's my wife Gloria. She's feeling under the weather."

Steve almost told the guy that he shouldn't be taking in strangers like this, but found himself inside and decided to drop it. Later, he'd bring it up with Maddie.

"Gloria! This man has news about Luke and your sister."

The blonde from the community center was underneath a quilt on the couch. Her cheeks were flushed and a box of tissues was on the floor by her. "My baby?"

"He's fine," Steve assured her quickly. "He's with Maddie in my hotel room. They're both safe."

The two exchanged glances. "Why aren't they

here? What happened?" Gloria's voice rose in panic. "They're not hurt, are they?"

"No. They're fine," Steve reassured them.

"We were told she rode off with a man on a motorcycle," John said.

"That would be me," Steve replied and told them basically what had happened so far without going into too much alarming detail. He'd only tell them if he had to.

"But why didn't you bring Luke and Maddie here?" Gloria asked.

Okay, so he had to. After telling them about the jacket, he added, "And the two guys have figured out you have it. I expect them to come here, and I thought it would be safer if Maddie kept your baby away."

"But I have two other babies!" Gloria looked like she was about to cry.

He hadn't realized there were other kids in the house, though with the way the Christmas tree was decorated with child-made ornaments, he probably should have. This complicated things. "If you let me see the jacket maybe I can figure out why everyone wants it."

"Oh, John, go get it! Hurry!" Gloria begged her husband and he quickly left the room.

Steve mentally crossed his fingers. At this point, he was hoping to find the coins—or something else—sewn into the lining of the jacket.

Removing the directions he'd written on the Lancaster notepad, he handed them to Gloria and pointed to the hotel's phone number. "You can reach Maddie here and talk to her."

He hoped Maddie would have the good sense not to alarm her sister.

"You said they knocked you out—has anyone looked at your head?"

Steve felt the lump on the back of his head. "It's okay. I've had worse."

His pulse quickened when John returned a few minutes later with an admittedly good-looking navy blazer.

"Mr. Jackson said we could call Maddie." Gloria gave her husband the information. "And while you're in the kitchen, would you be a love and make me some tea? My throat's still scratchy."

"Sure." John smiled at his wife in a way that hit Steve right between the eyes.

Love.

His father had never looked at his mother or anyone else that way.

And Steve knew in his heart that *he'd* never looked at anyone that way.

He couldn't watch. Instead he stared down at the blazer. It was an exclusive label with a first-class quality wool, but it was spoiled by cheap, plastic buttons. Details counted, something most people forgot.

He heard John leave to phone Maddie. "Tell her it shouldn't be much longer," Steve called after him.

He quickly squeezed the blazer all over, hoping finding the coins would be just that simple. Nothing. Not even the crackle of a secreted paper. He turned the blazer inside out and yanked on the lining.

At the sound of stitches ripping, Gloria protested. "Stop!"

Steve stopped.

"What are you doing?"

"I want to look in the lining."

"Well, you don't have to destroy it. Wait a minute." She looked behind her. "My sewing things are on the dining table. Can you bring me my basket?"

Steve saw a sewing machine and scraps of fabric that looked like the costume Maddie was wearing, along with glitter, cardboard, paints and glue. A sewing basket was on the floor beside the table leg. Steve brought the basket over to Gloria, who removed a wicked looking hooked tool and proceeded to neatly remove the stitches.

Neatly, but slowly.

Steve wanted to jerk it out of her hands, but didn't. Instead, he watched her work, finding a peacefulness stealing over him.

Inevitably, sitting there with nothing else to do, Steve compared the two sisters. Gloria, with the muted light shining behind her, sure was a looker, but Maddie had something she didn't, something infinitely more appealing. Steve wasn't sure what it was, but he knew he felt different. Alert and distracted at the same time. Edgier and calmer. What was it about Maddie? How could someone be appealing and exasperating at the same time?

She was more...aware somehow. More real. She talked more, too, he thought, smiling to himself.

And she also listens more.

She could be a friend, he thought. A good friend. The thought had barely formed before he remembered kissing her goodbye. He'd had to feel her in his arms once more. It hadn't been a choice.

In that moment, he acknowledged that platonic friendship with Maddie was out. With her, it was going to be all, or nothing.

"How much of the lining do I need to remove?" Gloria asked.

"Let me see." Relieved to stop puzzling over Maddie for the moment, Steve took the jacket and after checking the underside of the lining, studied the interfacing now revealed. It was a white fabric, perfect for writing on.

Only, he couldn't see anything. "Has the jacket been dry-cleaned?"

"A couple of times."

Maybe the cleaning removed or faded the writing. Steve stood and walked over to the lamp and chair by the window. Removing the shade, he held the jacket close to the bulb, searching for anything that Cortavilla might want. He hated to ask Gloria to rip more, or take out the interfacing, which would effectively ruin the jacket.

He heard the noise while he was standing by the window.

It might have been an animal in the bushes, but Steve doubted it. The curtains were drawn and probably revealed no more than shadows to anyone watching. Still pretending to study the inside of the jacket, Steve shifted his position and saw that he was standing in direct line of sight with the back door in the kitchen. It was half-paned with a sheer, gathered panel that was opened on the sides. He, and John, who was holding the telephone receiver to his ear, were visible to anyone.

The hair on the back of his neck bristled. Looking

around the room, the weapons available to him appeared to be several cardboard wrapping paper tubes, the lamp and the glass in the picture frame.

He knew without asking that these people didn't have a gun. Steve, himself, didn't carry a gun. He'd had enough of guns in his time and rarely found himself in a situation that demanded one.

Except now.

He waited, then relaxed. Cortavilla's men would have been inside long ago, which meant he was dealing with Frank and Murray—or an animal in the bushes.

Just then, John carried his wife's tea into the room, which gave Steve the opportunity to look in the direction of the kitchen. He didn't see anything outside the door.

But when John spoke, Steve forgot all about the door.

"I called the number you gave me, but there wasn't an answer in your room."

Steve made himself smile. "It's been quite an evening. Maddie's probably asleep."

He didn't believe it for a second.

LUKE WAS NOT impressed by luxury.

"You are your mother's child," Maddie murmured, though there was no way he'd hear her, since he was screaming.

She barely had time to look around before digging through the diaper bag for the bottle of formula. Once she found it and stuck on the nipple, she offered it to him and sat on a charming love seat.

Luke took a couple of pulls, turned his face away and cried.

"Hey, look, I know it's not warm, but can't you drink it anyway?"

No. Maddie went into the bathroom where Luke's cries bounced off the marble and were probably audible to every room in the hotel. She drew a sinkful of hot water and put the bottle into it. Then she paced.

And paced. She tried swaying, rocking, bouncing, changing him and even speaking to him in as deep a voice as she could. She brought out his favorite sock puppets Harry and Larry Yellow Eyes, but he wasn't having any of it.

Finally she retrieved the bottle and tried that again.

No luck. Luke was used to his mother's milk and obviously hated formula.

Maddie turned on the television, hoping that would drown out the crying, but from the accusatory looks the housekeeping staff that brought the crib gave her, knew she hadn't succeeded.

An eternity dragged by.

The concierge, himself, stopped by to see "if I may be of any service?" Maddie shook her head. "You've had complaints, haven't you?"

"There have been some strong expressions of concern," he allowed.

I'll bet. "Why don't I take him downstairs?" she offered and saw the relief in the man's eyes.

Maddie paced in the lobby in a circuit that rounded the Christmas tree, which didn't impress Luke, either.

She repeatedly tried giving him the bottle and all he'd done was dribble it out of his mouth so that the collar of his sleeper was soaked.

Between Luke's incessant crying and waiting to hear from Steve, Maddie's nerves were frayed.

She was also conscious of the averted looks by the hotel staff.

Miserably, she took Luke outside and paced by the doors. It had been well over an hour. Why hadn't Steve sent for her?

"Could you check and see if Mr. Jackson has left any messages for me?" she asked the doorman.

He called the front desk on a cell phone, then shook his head.

Maddie drew a deep breath. "Then will you please call me a taxi—and ask for one with a car seat."

8

STEVE HANDED THE jacket to Gloria. "I couldn't find anything. Could you go ahead and rip out the lining around the neck?" He watched her for a moment, then added casually, "While you're doing that, I'll give the hotel a call."

As he walked into the kitchen, Steve hoped he'd given a convincing performance. Maddie had better be there.

But she wasn't. Woody, the doorman, told Steve he'd called a taxi for her. "The kid was screaming. I hope she's a good tipper."

Maddie didn't have any money with her at all. "Check into it for me, will you Woody? If necessary, I'll cover it."

"Will do."

Great. Maddie was on her way over here. For all he knew, Frank and Murray were lurking in the shrubbery. Time to draw them and anyone else away from the house.

Now how did he explain what he needed to do to these gentle people?

He strode into the living room. Gloria glanced up and went back to her ripping. John sat on the floor beside the couch, apparently content to watch her.

Yeah, yeah. Very sweet.

"Okay, listen up." Steve assumed his commando stance, then softened it at their alarmed expressions. "Maddie and the baby are on their way over here. However, I believe the two men I told you about are here to break into your house and take this jacket." He gently removed it from a suddenly white-faced Gloria. "I'd like to draw them away from you and your children." He added the slightest stress to the word "children," hoping they wouldn't argue with him.

"We should call the police." John made as if to stand.

"No. We don't have time." Steve held up a hand to forestall any further questions or arguments. "I'll take care of the situation. Just ignore any noise you hear outside."

Gloria's hand crept toward her husband's.

"I *want* them to see me with this." He held up the jacket. "I want them to come after me, and not you. Do you understand?"

"But—"

"Let's keep the kids safe. Do you understand?" he repeated in a firmer voice.

They nodded.

"Okay. Tell Maddie...tell Maddie I'll be in touch."

He'd said the words before. But this time, he meant them. When he got to the front door, he turned and said, "Just play along."

Okay. Show time. He opened the door, turned to the frozen couple now sitting together on the couch and raised his hand as if in farewell. "Thank you very much *for giving me the jacket*." With Frank and

Murray, he figured he needed to spell things out. "You've been a big help."

He opened the screen door and stepped out onto the porch, stopping and refolding the jacket with its ripped lining over his arm. He heard nothing and saw no moving shadows. Well, what were they waiting for—a neon sign saying "Here it is"?

Steve cut across the grass making it easy for them to jump out at him. He reached the driveway where he'd parked his bike with still no sign of the two. Even Cortavilla's men would have jumped him by now.

He cut through the hedge lining the driveway and saw the car. Maddie's Honda. So that was it. They wanted to follow him.

So much the better. The farther away he could draw them, the safer Maddie and her family would be. Just one problem.

His bike tires were flat.

Well, that wasn't too smart of them, was it?

Steve draped the jacket across the seat and opened the flap of his leather tool kit to get the can of compressed air he kept for such situations. It wouldn't be enough to inflate both tires, but he could make the bike ridable until he found a gas station. Maybe that's when they'd make their move.

Kneeling down, he found the tire stem and was unscrewing the cap when he saw a moving shadow reflected in the chrome. He jerked to the left and the blow glanced off his shoulder, but it was enough to make him lose his balance and fall against the bike. He kicked out blindly and connected with a shin.

"Ow!" howled Murray. He dropped a piece of firewood and limped off.

These two were seriously grating on Steve's nerves as well as getting in far too many unanswered blows to his body.

"Moron! You were supposed to grab the jacket!" Frank yelled.

Take it already! Steve wanted to say, but knew if he didn't put up a token resistance, they'd wonder why.

Thus he found himself charging Frank, hoping Murray would run over to the bike, grab the jacket, and take off. Steve much preferred pursuing to being pursued.

It might have worked. In fact, it *was* working, except at that moment, Maddie's car, as though possessed, began honking its horn and flashing its lights.

LUKE CRIED ALL THE way home.

Maddie's eardrums were numb, but judging from the dirty looks the cab driver kept giving her in the rearview mirror, his eardrums were still functioning fully.

The cab turned onto her sister's street and Maddie gasped. There was her car, which meant Frank and Murray were already there.

Maddie ducked low and looked into the car as they drove past. From what she could tell, it was empty.

"Stop!"

"Gladly, lady." The driver jammed on the brakes.

"Back up to that car."

As he did so, Maddie looked all around. Her sister's house was three more houses down the block and she could see that the lights were on. But there was no sign of Steve's motorcycle.

She got out of the cab and carefully approached the car. The windows were down and it was unlocked. How dare they leave her car unlocked? Somebody might steal it—right.

Incredibly, there was her purse, still on the backseat next to Luke's car seat. Everything was in it, including her wallet. She paid the driver with her lunch money for the next week, and retrieved Luke. He quieted once he was back in her arms, but Maddie wasn't about to just walk up to her sister's house and leave the car here.

Her hands were shaking as she strapped Luke into the car seat. He didn't like his own any better than the last one and Maddie rolled up the windows in a vain hope that the noise wouldn't carry.

At the insistence of her parents, she had a spare car key in her wallet. Thankful now, she dug out the key and stuck it in the ignition, then tried feeding Luke the formula again.

It worked for about three minutes of blessed peace—long enough for Maddie to settle down and think.

It was while she was thinking that she saw Steve appear in the doorway. She considered letting him know she was there, but remembering his plan, decided to wait until he left, supposedly drawing the bad guys with him.

The thing was, she didn't see any bad guys and any minute she expected to see Frank and Murray at the very least.

The most was too scary to think about.

Though she was still a little fuzzy about what the scope of Steve's job entailed, Maddie was thankful he was helping them.

Assuming he *was* helping them.

He certainly took his time strolling across the lawn. Anyone who'd ever watched police dramas on television knew that this wasn't any way to act. He was right out in the open. Wouldn't Frank and Murray sense a trap?

Oh, that's right. "Frank and Murray" and "sense" didn't belong in the same sentence, although for stupid crooks, they'd been remarkably successful so far.

Steve had stopped and was looking at his bike. He laid something across the seat and began unbuckling a pouch on the side of the motorcycle.

And two shadows crept from behind the garage. One was tall with a cap, and the other short. Obviously Frank and Murray.

What should she do?

Nothing.

Steve was expecting them. He probably knew they were behind him right now. He was an expert, she reminded herself, and tried to forget that he'd already been hit in the head twice this evening.

And now a third time.

Maddie gasped and jerked the bottle out of Luke's mouth. She didn't recall Steve getting hit as being part of his plan. He'd fallen and it was two against one.

She saw him kick Murray and then come barreling toward Frank, but Murray had picked up something and was approaching.

Maddie couldn't stand it. She had to do something. She started the car, honked, and flashed the lights.

Murray froze, his shadow stretching on the white siding behind him.

Steve and Frank were still rolling on the ground. Since Steve was so much more muscular—very much more muscular...his arms stronger, his chest broader...

He must be in trouble. Putting the car into gear, Maddie drove forward and pulled into the driveway. She honked, but all that accomplished was to make Murray drop his stick, point at the car and yell.

Steve was on his back and Frank was sitting on his chest.

Maddie drove off the driveway, smashed through her sister's pansies, and headed straight toward Frank and Steve, honking all the while.

Good, she'd distracted them. Frank was actually scrambling to get out of the way, but it appeared Steve was trying to prevent him by holding onto his leg.

Maddie rolled down the window. "Let him go. It's not worth it!"

Steve shouted something back, but between Luke, the honking, and Murray's yelling, Maddie couldn't hear much.

Murray had taken off. Steve chased Frank, running to the motorcycle and flinging something after him. The two men didn't stop, but cut through Gloria's neighbor's yard.

Steve turned and came running toward Maddie. "What the *hell* are you doing?"

"Rescuing you!" she yelled back.

"I didn't want to be rescued! Don't you remember the plan?"

"It didn't look like the plan was going very well!"

He yanked open the driver's side door. "Scoot over. I'll drive."

Since it looked like he was prepared to sit on top of her if she didn't move, Maddie scooted.

But Steve didn't get in. Drawing his eyebrows together, he stared at the wailing Luke in the back. "What's wrong with him?"

"He doesn't like formula."

"But he drank it earlier."

"That wasn't formula."

"Then what was in the bottle—oh." Steve exhaled as he gazed at Luke. "Come here little guy." With a last look in the direction Frank and Murray had run, Steve opened the back door and unbuckled Luke. "Let's take you to your mom."

Leaving Maddie to trail behind, Steve scooped up Luke and took off for the house.

And this was the thanks she got?

She glared after him, but it was truly hard to remain angry with a man comforting a baby. Maddie grabbed the diaper bag and headed up the stairs after him.

She heard John and Gloria's excited voices before she saw them. Maddie reached the screen door in time to see Steve hand Luke to Gloria. "I know he's glad to see his mom."

"Not half as glad as his mom is to see him." Gloria sat up and began to unbutton her nightgown.

With a horrified expression, Steve whirled

around. Maddie was amused to see that the tops of his ears had reddened.

She slipped quietly inside and dropped the diaper bag beside the door.

Busy cooing over their son, John and Gloria didn't even look up. Maddie knew they must be incredibly relieved, but...didn't they wonder about her? She was a little hurt that they hadn't asked or noticed her come in.

She'd been the one to rescue their son and keep him safe—granted, she'd also been the one who allowed him to be kidnapped—but still.

They couldn't be angry—it wasn't her fault. Besides, Gloria and John never got angry. But Maddie did. She sighed. Just one more mark in the unworthy column.

She caught Steve looking at her. Talk about angry. "What?"

He jerked his head toward the kitchen and Maddie followed him in there. He held the door for her, then carefully shut it.

Maddie wasn't fooled. Not only was the guy not appreciative of her efforts on his behalf, he was royally ticked off.

"I thought I told you to stay at the hotel," he began in an forbidding undertone.

"I tried staying at the hotel, but Luke wouldn't stop crying. And even then, when I found my car, I waited in it until I saw *you* in trouble." She went to the cabinet above the sink and got down two glasses. "What would you have done if I hadn't rescued you? Huh? Tell me that."

"I didn't need rescuing! I was putting up a token resistance—"

"You were getting beaten up!"

"By *Frank?*" He gave a disbelieving laugh.

"No, by Murray with the stick."

"Okay, so he landed a lucky hit."

Maddie raided Gloria's refrigerator for orange juice. "He was getting ready to land several lucky hits." She poured two glasses and handed him one. "How are you, anyway?"

Steve rubbed his shoulder. "I've had worse."

"Gloria keeps aspirin in cabinet above the telephone table." Maddie opened the door. "Want one?"

"Just give me the bottle," Steve grumbled.

Maddie watched as he poured out a few. "Just admit it—things didn't work out the way you intended."

"Not after you repossessed their getaway car, no." He tossed the aspirin in his mouth.

"Oh." She hadn't thought about that.

Maddie sipped her juice, watching as he drained his glass in one long swallow.

"Yeah, oh. How did you think they were going to leave?"

"I didn't notice that they had any problem leaving."

Steve gave her a dark look. It went with the rest of him. His black scruffiness contrasted with her sister's yellow and green country kitchen, and he seemed bigger than she remembered. Almost too big for the wooden ladder-back chairs around the breakfast table.

Maddie thought he looked great. She sighed. He wasn't the type of man she was supposed to think looked great.

The kitchen was cozy and warm. In fact, Maddie was warm for the first time in hours. Too warm. Setting her glass on the counter, she pointed to the laundry room off the kitchen. "I'm getting out of this costume."

Once inside the little room, Maddie pulled up the hem of her robe and tugged the scratchy fabric over her head. Digging around in the laundry basket, she found one of Gloria's T-shirts, put it on and stepped back into the kitchen. "I am *glad* to be out of this."

She turned the costume right side out and noticed the dirt stains around the hem. Even though it would look more authentic for the play, Maddie figured she'd better try to sponge them out.

Steve hadn't said anything and she glanced up as she walked past him to the sink. He was staring at her, but not in the angry way he had earlier.

"What?"

"Nothing." He visibly swallowed. "I'm...I'm going outside and get the jacket." He edged toward the kitchen door as he spoke. "Unless Frank and Murray came back for it, or someone else..." He pushed open the door. "I'll be right back."

What was that all about? Maddie looked down at herself. She was wearing jeans and Gloria's wrinkled blue East Street Angels basketball team T-shirt. Very nondescript.

Certainly nothing that would attract the notice of a man like Steve Jackson.

STEVE PRACTICALLY TRIPPED over his feet in his haste to get away from the vision that was Maddie.

Maddie was a woman.

This was not news to him. He'd even kissed her. Several times.

And yet...*Maddie was a woman.* Somehow, it had hit him hard right then. One second he'd been mad as fire at her and the next, she'd taken off that costume and *pow.* Reality had hit harder than Murray.

It was the jeans and the T-shirt. Maybe just the T-shirt.

Steve forced himself to pay attention to his surroundings and quit thinking about Maddie as a woman as he walked across the lawn, but there was no sign of Frank and Murray or anyone else.

The jacket was caught on the hedge separating Maddie's sister's house from the neighbors. Steve shook his head when he saw it. Those two goofs couldn't manage to do anything right.

Steve righted his motorcycle and pushed it closer to the house before snagging the jacket and walking on around to the kitchen door.

He caught sight of Maddie at the sink, scrubbing at her costume. She looked so...so normal. Incredibly normal. Alluring in a way the women in the clubs he went to weren't. Not particularly thin, but not fat, either. She had hips she probably thought were too big, but weren't, and breasts that she probably thought were too small, but...but knowing Maddie, she probably didn't think that way.

During the time they were together, he'd heard a lot of the way she thought. He'd told her a lot of his thoughts, too, and she hadn't run screaming from him. There hadn't been any place she could run, so maybe that wasn't a true test.

She was different. Maybe that was part of her attraction. He remembered how easily she'd ridden behind him on the motorcycle and knew she hadn't gotten that experience teaching Sunday School.

He was going to have to do something about Maddie, or rather his feelings for her.

It would help considerably if he knew what those feelings were. Maddie was a good girl—woman, he corrected. She wasn't his usual type at all, and a man just didn't mess around with good women the way he might with other women.

Maybe it was because he knew she was capable of lapsing.

Anytime Steve thought he was in danger of feeling more than a surface attraction to a woman, he spent time with her. Lots of time. True it was usually in bed, but afterward, he'd had enough. Now, tempting as it was, he couldn't do that with Maddie.

But Maddie was dangerous in a different way—the white-picket-fence way—and Steve was not going through that horror again. So it would seem the solution would be to mire himself in domesticity. Behind the kitchen door he'd closed, he knew Gloria, John and Luke made about as domestic a trio as he was ever likely to find.

"Sometimes I amaze myself," he murmured as the perfect solution presented itself.

"The jacket was still out there," he said as he opened the door.

"Frank and Murray didn't look like they intended

to come back." Maddie used her shoulder to push hair out of her eyes.

"Here, let me." Before he thought twice, Steve reached out and tucked the piece of hair behind her ear. It would be so easy to curl his fingers around the side of her face and draw her closer—

"Thanks." She went back to cleaning the costume. "What happens now?"

"Now I apologize for jumping all over you earlier." Not the best choice of words.

She glanced up at him and turned on the faucet. "You don't have to."

"I want to."

"Why?"

Why? She was asking why? This wasn't the way the conversation was supposed to go. "Because I— why are you asking me why? Can't you just accept the apology?"

Maddie turned off the faucet and inspected the wet blotch on the costume. "You don't strike me as a man who likes to apologize."

"Does anyone?"

"I suppose not."

She'd gone all distant on him and damned if he knew why. Women.

"So now that I've ruined your great and wonderful plan, what happens?"

Steve looked down at the jacket and the lining hanging out of it. "I think up a new plan."

"I take it that means you didn't find your gold doubloons or whatever you were looking for."

He shook his head. "Couldn't find anything in the jacket, either."

She got a hand towel out of a drawer, then turned to face him as she blotted the water from the costume. "I don't suppose any new plan involves calling the police?" Her eyes were a bright, challenging blue.

"Not yet."

Maddie slapped the towel against the counter. "My sister and her family are in danger! I will not have you risking their safety just so you can collect a reward for some gold coins."

"I don't want them at risk, either," Steve assured her. "That's why I'm going to stay right here until this whole thing has been solved."

9

"AUNT MADDIE?"

A little hand that smelled like grape jelly patted her face.

"Wha'?" Maddie was in a *Lion King* sleeping bag on the floor between her nephews' beds and she wanted to stay there at least two more hours.

"Aunt Maddie, there's a very grumpy man on our sofa."

"Yah!" echoed another voice just a little past her morning brightness threshold.

"And there's a very grumpy Aunt Maddie in here."

"Yah!"

Maddie had no warning before a laughing lump of two-year-old nephew landed on her rib cage. "Ohh, Mark...let Aunt Maddie go back to sleep."

"No!" He bounced as Maddie tried to burrow farther into the sleeping bag.

Giggling wildly, Mark pulled on the edge of the bag. Maddie gave a mock growl.

"Aunt Maddie...what about the grumpy man?"

Maddie opened her sleep-deprived eyes to stare into the overly serious ones of her oldest nephew, Matthew. "Is he asleep?"

"He *was*."

"Did you talk to him?"

Matthew violently shook his head. "He's a *stranger.*"

Technically, Maddie supposed that's what Steve was, but yesterday's shared experiences had been the equivalent of a total immersion getting-to-know-you course. "What did your dad tell you about him?"

"Dad's in the shower and Mommy has a sick throat."

Before this was over, they'd all get the flu, Maddie supposed. "The grumpy man is friend of Aunt Maddie's."

"Is he your soot'ble life partner?"

Maddie blinked.

Matt continued. "I hope so, 'cause Mommy and Daddy want you to find a soot'ble life partner."

Oh, they did, did they? Her nephew was a never-ending source of information and a little busybody to boot.

She tickled Mark until he collapsed into giggles and rolled off her. Then, she sat up. "Mr. Jackson is just a friend." A pang went through her at the word "friend." "He might stay here with you for a few days."

Matthew didn't look very happy at the prospect. "He's *very* grumpy."

"We didn't get much sleep last night." Maddie heard noises from the kitchen. "Have you two had breakfast?"

"Dad made us jelly toast."

"Yah!"

"Okay...well, scoot while Aunt Maddie gets dressed. Then we'll all go visit the grumpy man."

"We're going to spy on him," Matthew announced.

"Good. Report back to me."

Matthew took his brother's hand and crept down the hall. Maddie figured she had about a minute and a half before their "report."

She wiggled out of the sleeping bag and dragged on her jeans. She was tying her shoelaces when a self-righteous Matthew returned, his hands over Mark's ears.

"He said a bad word," Matthew reported.

Poor Steve. Maddie took her other shoe and headed for the kitchen. She caught herself on the threshold, the kids clinging to her legs. Steve's hair was wild, his beard darkened his face and, yes, he was *very* grumpy.

"What are you looking at?" he growled at them.

"I've had reports of a savage in the kitchen."

He was opening the aspirin bottle, and after a quick glance at the two boys behind her, obviously tempered his voice. "I'm not a morning person. So sue me."

Maddie lifted her chin. "If you can't control your language, then you're going to have to spend your mornings elsewhere."

Surprise flitted across his face. "There is no coffee in this house," he grumbled.

"Herbal tea."

He looked pained. Popping the aspirin in his mouth, he downed them with a glass of water. "So what's the schedule around here?"

Maddie sat at the kitchen table and put on her other shoe. Matthew and Mark watched from the doorway. "John spends half a day working at Social Services, then will go to the center. Since Gloria's sick, she'll stay home today. School is out for Christmas break, so I thought I'd stay here and help with the kids."

He nodded. "Nobody but John leaves the house, understand?"

"Do you really think..." She deliberately trailed off, not wanting Matthew, the human sponge to worry his mother by reporting snippets of conversation.

Steve seemed to understand. "Yes, I really think. They didn't get what they came for last night."

Maddie finished tying her shoe and caught sight of her reflection in the toaster. *Her* hair wasn't anything to brag about, either. She casually finger-combed it, but stopped when she saw that Steve was watching her.

"I'm going out." Abruptly, he set his glass on the counter and strode through the kitchen. Matthew and Mark scurried out of the way. "I'll be back."

NOW HE WAS TERRIFYING little kids.

Hell, he was terrifying himself. Maddie, all sleep tousled and surrounded by kids, had unleashed yearnings he'd thought were burned out long ago.

Not good. Not good at all.

So, change of plans. He would not spend the morning working at the hotel. He would pack his computer and hightail it back to the house and over-dose on domesticity.

If he couldn't burn out his feelings, then he'd drown them out.

AFTER THREE UNDILUTED hours with the boys, Maddie decided that the person who had coined the phrase "domestic bliss" was first of all, male, and second, far away in a luxurious hotel ordering from room service at the time.

How did Gloria *stand* it? And how could Maddie ever have felt she wanted it? A roomful of kindergarteners was nothing compared to her nephews.

She couldn't even risk sending the rambunctious Matthew and Mark outside to play. The weather was glorious—cool and sunny—but mindful of Steve's warnings, she didn't dare let them even into the backyard until he returned.

Her mother had been by with a change of clothes and the news that the dress rehearsal had been rescheduled for tomorrow night and "Could Maddie please be on time?"

When Maddie pointed out that her car had been stolen and she'd been locked up, her mother had looked at her with sympathy. "You must learn to manage situations better, Magdalyn."

"Mom!"

"The two men came to the center last night and explained everything. It was all a misunderstanding."

"Did they tell you they locked Luke and me, and Steve, the man who helped us, in a storage shed?"

"You frightened them."

Maddie would have pointed out that she'd been frightened, too, except that would have triggered the "faith and fear" sermon. "Did they tell you about the jacket?"

"Yes, and we sent them here, but it was late, so I imagine they'll come by for it this morning."

But, of course they'd come by last night. Maddie rubbed her temple. Nothing she could say to her mother would make any difference. Her parents had always lived openly and trustingly. When that trust had seemingly been violated, they accepted it, forgave and moved on.

I must be a changeling, Maddie thought, looking at her mother's sweetly serene face.

"It's good that you are able to help your sister today, though we miss you both at the center." Her mother sighed with the nearest to a frown that she ever managed. "The clinic is full today." She brightened. "But Dr. Hardesty has brought an intern with him to help. So you see, everything works out." Serenity restored, Maddie's mother went to the bedroom to speak with Gloria, then left for the center.

Steve returned shortly thereafter, and that's when Maddie's tenuous serenity unraveled.

Since John and Gloria didn't have a television, Maddie decided on a big Christmas decoration-making project. Some of the homemade paper ornaments on the tree in the living room were looking faded and torn and Gloria hadn't made popcorn strings yet this year.

On second thought, Matthew and Mark with needles didn't sound like a good idea, so Maddie settled on dough ornaments, something Gloria would object to if she knew about it ahead of time, since it was wasting flour.

Sometimes Maddie thought a little waste was good for people.

She and the boys were having a good time kneading food coloring into the salt and flour mixture when Steve knocked on the kitchen door and let himself in.

Maddie, holding a lump of green dough, stared. This definitely wasn't the same Steve who had left that morning.

He'd shaved, for one thing, and had abandoned the all-black look for khaki and a pale blue denim button-down shirt.

For another, he smiled and Maddie's throat went dry.

She'd kissed that mouth and that mouth had kissed hers.

She sighed, knowing it had been in another time in another place and he'd already moved on.

"Aunt Maddie, Mark used up all the red!"

Maddie jerked her attention away from Steve to find Mark holding an empty bottle of red food dye. Taking it away before he could put it in his mouth, she reassured Matthew that they now had plenty of red dough and that Mark would share.

"But I want purple and red is a part of purple."

Maddie pinched off an intensely colored piece of Mark's red dough.

"No!" He swiveled the rest of the lump away from her, but Maddie had what she needed.

"Take some of the blue dough—not all of it—and mix this in."

Matthew looked skeptical, but mashed the lumps

together, his frown smoothing when a muddy purple formed.

The entire time, Maddie was aware that Steve was silently watching.

"Looks like fun," he said.

"You're welcome to join in," Maddie offered, never dreaming that he'd actually do so.

"Okay. Then we can break for lunch." Holding up a basket, he smiled. "I had the hotel chef fix a few things. Thought maybe the munchkins there might be getting a little cabin crazy and would enjoy a picnic."

Was this the same man who'd frightened her nephews this morning? Was this the same man, period? Maddie stared at him as he set the basket on the counter, then took his duffel bag and coat into the other room.

When he returned, he'd unbuttoned his sleeves and was rolling up the cuffs.

He was serious. He was really sitting at the table. He was actually taking a piece of Matthew's blue salt dough and rolling it between his palms. "Now, how does this stuff work?"

An hour later, they'd produced one Christmas tree with ornaments, a yellow snake, a lumpy purple lamb, and a blue classic 1918 Powerplus solo motorcycle with V-twin engines.

Steve had been great with the kids. They seemed to have forgotten that he was the "grumpy" man of this morning, and laughed and shrieked so loud that Gloria had called out to them, which made everyone giggle and talk in stage whispers for about two minutes.

Maddie was enjoying herself—too much, because as she caught Steve's eye across the table, she started wishing for things that couldn't be.

Right after they put the ornaments in the oven to bake, Luke woke up and a stunned Maddie found herself nodding when Steve offered to change him and take him to Gloria while Maddie cleaned up the boys and put away the leftover dough.

Darn it, why *couldn't* this man be Maddie's "soot'ble" life partner?

STEVE KEPT WAITING for boredom to settle in, but he'd gotten a kick out of modeling the motorcycle. He hoped Maddie didn't burn it up in the oven.

But the idea wasn't to be having fun. The idea was to not have fun. Was there anything worse than changing a baby's diapers? That's why he'd volunteered.

But the anticipated revulsion just didn't happen. Luke was a mess, too. But Steve found it was similar to tending wounds during a mission that hadn't gone according to plan. It had to be done, so he did it and didn't think about the details of what he was doing.

"Hey, there, bud."

Steve was gratified when Luke stopped crying to stare at his face. "Big day yesterday, right? Well, your mom's waiting for you, so you don't have to worry about the food supply."

With one hand on Luke's stomach to keep him from rolling off the tabletop, Steve looked in a drawer and found a whole pile of the stretchy pajamas with feet like the baby had been wearing yester-

day. Little clowns, little bunnies and birdies and...
"Luke, buddy, your wardrobe. We gotta talk." Steve
found one of the outfits decorated with trains and
decided to dress Luke in that. "Sorry about the smi-
ley faces on the engines. It looks like the best we've
got. No wonder your oldest bro is turning into an old
woman. Mark's the one to watch out for, though.
That kid is fearless."

Steve finished snapping the outfit and picked up
Luke to take him into Gloria.

"How are you feeling?" he asked her as he tapped
on the open door.

Gloria put aside the book she was reading.
"Guilty," she said and reached for Luke. "I'm lots
better and here I am, just lazing away the day."

"Don't feel guilty. Maddie and I are doing fine.
Take advantage of the break and get completely
well."

"Thank you." She smiled the purest smile Steve
had ever seen. "You're a good man."

He actually felt his heart squeeze. "I'm not, but
thanks for saying so."

LUNCH WAS FUN, and the food was spectacular,
though not fully appreciated by a five-year-old and a
two-year-old. Not only that, the sandwiches didn't
have crusts. Gloria would have a cow at the waste if
she knew, and she would because Maddie knew
Matthew would tell her.

"You don't have to eat the chicken curry sandwich
if you don't want to," Maddie told her nephews
when she saw their faces after a few bites.

"But that's wasteful," Matt told her, grimacing as

he attempted to chew another mouthful. "We should be grateful to have food."

Maddie exchanged a look with Steve. "You don't have to be that grateful." She took the sandwiches out of reach.

"There's plenty of the ham," Steve said and pushed the basket toward the boys, who looked as though they couldn't believe they didn't have to continue eating the sandwiches they didn't like.

"My family is of the clean-plate school," Maddie told Steve.

"And you?"

"Sometimes I skip school," she admitted with a grin.

The sandwiches may not have been a hit, but the cookies... Beautifully decorated sugar cookies with fanciful scenes of Christmas and a snowy winter such as the boys would never see here in Houston.

Maddie hated to bite into hers, but nobody else had that problem.

After lunch, Steve played catch with Matthew and pushed Mark in his swing, his shrieks of "Higher!" reverberating through the neighborhood.

It was all very domestic. Some might even say blissful.

Maddie would not be one of them. She was ready to tear her hair out.

She could hardly wait for nap time. How could Steve manage to interact with her nephews without a hint of impatience? Maddie couldn't imagine living day after day like this. Yes, the circumstances were unusual, but she was about to go crazy.

It didn't help that Steve had apparently placed

himself in the running for the Perfect Man Award. The crabbier Maddie got, the more se—oh, good grief, she'd thought of the word "serene" in connection with Steve.

Her family had infected him while she carried a natural immunity. And she wasn't talking about the flu.

Finally, their after-lunch play wound down and Maddie shooed the boys off for nap time.

"I don't take naps anymore," Matthew announced, then amended his statement when he saw his aunt's face. "But I pretend so Mark will go to sleep."

"Pretend for at least an hour, okay?" Maddie handed him a book and tucked the covers under Mark's chin. Bless him, his eyes were already closed.

She found Steve hooking up a laptop computer to the kitchen phone line. As she watched, he removed the curious electronic card from his wallet and shoved it into a slot in the machine. It didn't look like a computer disk, but Maddie supposed that's what it was.

"Working on secret stuff?" she asked.

"No secrets. I sent out some inquiries this morning and I want to see what info has come in."

Ah, at last something to break up the tedium of the day.

What a horrible thought! In spite of the ordinariness of their activities, they were still in danger, and here she was actually looking forward to the excitement it would bring to her life.

How pathetic.

Why couldn't she find the same contentment her

parents and John and Gloria did? Did they fight these selfish thoughts?

Did Gloria *ever* want a new dress—not a different one, a *new* one that someone else hadn't worn first? Even her wedding dress had come from the thrift shop.

Oh, the dress had been beautiful and had probably been very expensive, and of course nobody noticed that the bride who'd worn it before Gloria had probably caught her heel on the underskirt and torn it because nobody saw the underskirt.

Except Maddie and her mother. Her mother had repaired it with blue thread, keeping with the "something borrowed, something blue" custom. It was a sweet thought, but...

But Maddie had to get over this dissatisfaction and the subsequent guilt.

The man sitting at her sister's telephone table didn't look like the type to feel guilt about anything. He moved through life confident of his place in it.

And Maddie wouldn't mind moving through a little of it with him. She smothered a sigh.

"Kids asleep?" he asked.

"Yes, or as good as." Maddie watched his fingers move over the computer keys. He had nice fingers. But then, he pretty much had nice everything.

"Can I help?" The offer popped out of her mouth before she could stop it. Of course there was nothing she could do to help. She just...okay, she just wanted to hang around Steve.

There truly was no hope for her.

Without glancing up at her, Steve answered. "Yes, there is something. Your sister took apart that jacket and I looked at it, but I couldn't find anything. Before she sews the lining up again, do suppose you could give it a once-over?"

"Sure!"

The jacket was with Gloria's sewing things on the dining table. Maddie retrieved it and returned to the kitchen.

She was probably being adolescently transparent, but she didn't care.

MADDIE WOULDN'T FIND anything in the jacket, and she probably knew it. Steve was just grateful she played along with him.

He enjoyed having her around. Yesterday, if Mama Garcia had served him her burritos and then told him how he'd be spending the next day, he'd never have believed her.

He didn't believe himself.

He knew his contentment wouldn't last—he was surprised it had lasted this long. The kids were cute, but he'd seen cute kids before. That didn't explain the actual fun he'd had with them or the warm fuzzies he got watching Maddie surreptitiously try to undo their teaching. He wondered if she knew what she was doing and decided that she probably did. With her as their aunt, they'd turn out okay.

"I couldn't see anything but lint," Maddie reported. "If the coins were hidden in there, they're gone now."

"Yeah, I figured as much." He risked a look at her and found she was sitting closer than he'd thought. "You can give it back to your sister to sew up again."

"Do you think Frank and Murray will come back here for it?"

He didn't want to think about Frank and Murray. "Unfortunately."

"Then what do we do?"

Several inappropriate ideas occurred to him. Steve exhaled as his e-mail downloaded. "We wrap it up with a great big bow, tell them Merry Christmas, and give it to them."

Nodding, she left the room. He watched her go, wondering how jeans and a sweater had become so sexy.

When Maddie returned, she pulled a kitchen chair up beside him. "Do you mind if I watch?"

"There's not much to see." *Don't go away.*

"What's on the screen now?"

She'd pulled her chair so close he could feel the warmth of her body. "A link to pawnshop inventories in the area." Naturally, the most tedious part of his job. She'd leave now for sure.

Maddie wrinkled her forehead. "When were the doubloons stolen?"

She looked cute with wrinkles. "Nearly three years ago. I'm just checking pawnshops in case Frank and Murray got lucky today." *I would like to get lucky today.*

Down boy. Steve swallowed and searched his database of coin dealers, trying to ignore Maddie and her wrinkles and her sweater and her subversive parenting.

"Look!" She reached across him and pointed to the screen. "Gold doubloons!"

Her excited face was just inches away from his.

Steve kept his gaze glued to the screen. "Wrong date and wrong galleon wreck. They've been listed ever since I started checking."

"Oh." Her disappointment was endearing.

Everything about her was pretty much endearing. *This way lies misery, Jackson.*

He fought the urge to touch her. Things were cooler today and he didn't need to be heating them up again.

She leaned forward to read something on the screen and he had to grit his teeth as her hair brushed against his shoulder.

If he didn't touch her, he might very well go nuts.

IF HE DIDN'T TOUCH her, she'd go nuts.

Okay, so she hadn't actively flirted in a month of Sundays. Was she that rusty?

Or was he that resistant?

Or was she too subtle?

Her mother had brought her a red sweater with white reindeer on it that had been donated to the center's thrift shop because the red had bled into the white and the reindeer now had pink heads and antlers.

It was not a good flirting outfit.

Maddie sighed.

She was only kidding herself that a couple of pity kisses equaled interest on this man's part.

Look at him. He was ruggedly handsome with enough maturity on his features to make them interesting without being pretty.

He had a small scar that disappeared into his right eyebrow and creases around his eyes when he smiled—which wasn't often. He'd shaved and re-vealed a squarish jaw. Without his beard, she could see that he gritted his teeth a lot. Like now.

She was probably getting on his nerves. Backing away, she tried to look interested in the lists scrolling across the computer screen.

STEVE SINCERELY HOPED that the doubloons hadn't shown up on any dealer's "buy" list because he wasn't reading a thing.

This was pointless. All he wanted to do was forget doing the right thing and go for a few minutes of wrong.

"How did you get to do what you're doing?" Maddie asked.

"You mean looking for lost and stolen property?"

She nodded. "Were you like a private detective, or something?"

"No. I was in the army." Talking was good. Talking would distract him. He told her about his stint in the military and afterward in the security business, and the first time he found stolen property. "After that, I started freelancing. My wife didn't like it," he added. "I wasn't around much."

"Did she ever go with you?"

Not all jobs were dangerous, but it had never oc-curred to him to take Celia with him. "She wouldn't have been interested."

"Did you ever ask her?"

Steve shook his head. "Actually, by then, I wanted to get away from her." The admission didn't make him look very good.

Well, maybe he didn't want to look good to her.

Maybe he wanted her to make some polite comment and go off and do whatever normal people did during the day.

He'd never been able to figure it out. His childhood had been a nightmare and marriage hadn't felt normal, either. Moving around and doing something different all the time felt normal.

Angry with himself, he punched a key and the scrolling stopped. He typed in a new command and an FBI screen appeared.

"What's *that?*"

Steve typed in his password, and gained access to the records area he wanted.

"Uh...should I be seeing this?"

"Probably not."

"Cool."

That made him smile, which made him want to kiss her all over again.

So when she smiled back, he did.

As soon as his lips touched hers—actually as soon as he'd known he was going to kiss her—Steve knew it wasn't a good idea.

That was too many kisses for her to ignore, not that she was ig— He inhaled sharply as Maddie wound her arms around him and landed in his lap.

The chair was just a small wooden side chair and his arms were full of Maddie. He had to hold on tightly to keep her centered or they'd tip over.

His whole body sighed as she demonstrated what an apt pupil she'd become in the art of kissing.

Steve liked kissing but had found that not many of the women he'd seen in the past couple of years liked to kiss. Usually he had to talk them into it and they were always glad he had, but...

Steve didn't want to think about them anymore. He didn't want to think about Celia anymore, either.

There was only Maddie and her mouth and tongue.

And fingers.

And teeth.

A Maddie who was about to surpass the teacher.

A Maddie who was unbuttoning his shirt.

He caught her hands. "Hey...this probably isn't a good idea."

"Probably not." She kissed his throat.

He could hardly breathe.

Maddie licked his ear.

Turning his head he nuzzled the side of her neck. "Maddie..." he whispered. "Where are you going with this?"

She drew back, her cheeks flushed. "Where do you want to go?"

So sweetly tempting. He shook his head. "I'm not the one for you."

"Can't I decide that?"

"No."

"Why not?"

"Maddie, you're a good girl—"

She gave a bitter laugh that didn't fit her personality. "*No*, I'm not."

He looked at her, then kissed her hands before drawing them away from his shirt. Somewhere out there was a professor Steve wanted to meet in a dark alley after class. "The guy was a jerk. He took advantage of your inexperience."

"So now I'm experienced."

"Not experienced enough."

She leaned forward and walked her fingers up his chest. "That's where *you* come in."

"You'll get hurt."

"That's my problem."

"*I'll* get hurt."

When she drew back and looked at him in surprise, he realized what he'd said.

They were both very still for several seconds and then, instead of continuing to argue, or worse, realizing victory was at hand, Maddie moved off his lap. He wished she'd say something. Most women would have said something. Why was it she never acted the way she was supposed to?

She wasn't even looking at him. Pointing to his monitor, she said, "You have a message."

He refocused on the computer and clicked over to the message screen. It was a whole file full of information on Enrique Cortavilla.

Including the fact that he'd been missing for nearly three years.

10

IF MADDIE HADN'T been trying to be cool and sophisticated and show Steve that she could turn her feelings off and on just like he could...if she hadn't pointed out the message...well, she didn't know what, but things would probably be a lot different by now.

She'd be well and truly a fallen women instead of one who'd just tripped.

Instead, one minute Steve was kissing her and the next he'd completely forgotten she was there. Or at least it seemed that way. He typed fast and furiously, made phone calls after putting the little electronic gizmo in her sister's phone, and suddenly, it was okay to call the police if they saw any suspicious characters lurking about.

Maddie had to admit that she got over being miffed fairly quickly once things started happening. She'd searched files for Steve while he was on the telephone and, well, it was pretty heady stuff—like realizing the giant jigsaw puzzle you'd been working on actually had all the pieces for once.

She even, by herself, found a huge piece of the puzzle. She'd been reading investigator's notes about Cortavilla and came across the information that he was in the habit of giving his trusted lieutenants a gold Spanish doubloon. Each was different and became an identifying marker.

Steve gave a low whistle. "No wonder he wants the ones that were stolen. I'll bet you that the key to what coin went to which lieutenant was in that book Frank and Murray were supposed to take."

"Then do you think the coins were in the jacket and somewhere between the time Frank and Murray took it and the center got it, the coins were taken out?" Maddie asked. She was making coffee with the coffeemaker and beans that Steve had brought from his hotel room.

"Or they were never taken at all and Cortavilla used the theft as an excuse to put in a claim and then used the insurance money to finance his withdrawal to Mexico."

"Then why does he want the jacket back?"

"Good point."

Maddie poured two mugs of coffee, liberally lacing hers with milk and sugar. "Can't we just give the jacket to the police?"

Grimly, he shook his head. "There's nothing in that jacket. Cortavilla will assume we've got possession of whatever it is they're looking for—and I'm assuming it *is* the coins. What I want to do is direct him away from you and your family."

"How?"

Steve wrapped his hands around the mug and leaned on his elbows. "Let Frank and Murray get the jacket back before Cortavilla realizes it's here. Right now, he thinks Frank and Murray can lead him to the coins. Obviously, he was willing to wait until they were released from prison since he's been lying low since the theft."

"Do you think Frank and Murray know what they've done?"

Steve shook his head. "They didn't at first, but they do now."

Right after that Matt and Mark woke up, but during the hour Maddie had spent working with Steve, she felt as though she'd come home. She actually enjoyed doing the stuff Steve claimed was tedious. She liked reading the reports looking for clues. She loved discussing possible scenarios.

She thought they made a good team.

Did he?

BY REHEARSAL TIME the next night, Frank and Murray still hadn't made their move.

Maddie was glad, because it meant she'd spent another day with Steve, even though she had to practically chain Gloria to the bed and make more sock puppets with Matt and Mark.

However, Gloria had pronounced herself well enough to attend the Christmas pageant rehearsal in her rightful role and Maddie, though glad her sister was well, selfishly regretted not having an excuse to hang around her house instead of going back to work at the center.

Steve had shown her another kind of life. How was she going to bear it when he left?

John had gone ahead to the rehearsal with Matthew, who was a lamb, and Mark, who was with a group of other younger children dressed as angels so they could sit in the front and see the play.

Maddie was going to drive Gloria and Luke, and Steve planned to follow on his motorcycle, then surreptitiously circle back and keep an eye on the house for Frank and Murray.

They were nearly ready to leave when the doorbell rang.

"Get that for me, will you, Maddie?" Gloria called from Luke's room.

"Shall I answer it?" Maddie whispered to Steve.

Holding up a hand, he moved toward the window and peered out onto the darkened street. "Older model...dark—maybe a Chevy sedan?"

"Sounds like my parents' car."

Still, Steve motioned for her to wait until he pressed himself next to the wall beside the door, then nodded.

It was probably nothing, yet Maddie's heart pounded. Wishing her sister's door had a peephole, she opened it a crack and looked out through the screen door.

Frank and Murray stared back at her.

She gasped. Steve stepped in front of her and yanked the door the rest of the way open.

"Hey, we don't want no trouble!" Frank proclaimed backing up.

"It's a little late for that!" Maddie said from behind Steve.

"I'll handle this," he said. "What do you want?"

"Magdalyn, what is going on?" A third man stood to the side.

Maddie peered around Steve. "Daddy?"

DADDY?

Steve stepped out of the way as the man he now

recognized as the Preacher Givens opened the door and gestured for Frank and Murray to enter.

"I don't know whose influence you've been under," he said with a cool look at Steve, "but this is not the way you've been taught to greet your fellow man."

"They're the men who stole my car!"

Frank dug in his pocket and produced Maddie's keys. "Forgot we had 'em," he mumbled.

"They had need of transportation," Maddie's father said as though that justified everything.

"Luke was in the back. They locked us in a storage place down by the ship channel!"

"You frightened them."

Maddie cast a disgusted look at Frank and Murray. "With what? Lamb costumes?"

"Magdalyn." Maddie's father looked sad.

"I'm sorry." She stared at the floor.

Steve felt an old anger stirring within him. Maddie's father's self-righteous unreasonableness was as bad in its way as his father's yelling abusiveness had been. Maybe even more so since it was cloaked in good intentions.

"With all due respect, sir," he began, "these men are known criminals—"

"Who have paid their debt to society," Preacher Givens gently interrupted. "Society should now welcome them back."

How could she live with this? Steve glanced over at Maddie who didn't meet anyone's eyes. Even Frank and Murray looked uncomfortable.

"Daddy, is that you?" Gloria, garbed in the costume Maddie had worn the other day, carried Luke into the living room. "Shouldn't you be at the rehearsal?"

At the sight of Gloria, Maddie's father's face turned mushy. "Your mother has everything well under control. I just try to stay out of the way."

"Oh, Daddy!"

Well, it was obvious who daddy's little girl was.

As Preacher Givens made nice with Gloria, Steve glared at the two men.

"I just want my jacket," Murray whined.

Steve caught Maddie's eye and nodded.

"It's in here." Maddie went to the front coat closet.

"Mother said you two might come by for it," Gloria said as though they were just anybody from the center.

Steve felt as though he was in some parallel universe. How had Maddie's family managed to survive all this time?

Maddie, that's how. Maddie knew what was up, but her family didn't. Even now, she might be casually handing over the jacket, but he sensed a wary readiness about her. If Frank and Murray made a wrong move, she'd be ready to act.

He liked that about her. He liked that a lot.

Gloria had finished sewing the lining back, Steve saw. Murray, his face lit nearly as bright as the Christmas tree, reached for the jacket.

Then he frowned. "This isn't the one."

"It isn't?" Steve asked sharply.

"It doesn't look the same."

"I had to repair it," Gloria said smoothly. "Here." She slipped it from its hanger. "Try it on."

He did and Steve had to endure everyone—but Maddie—admiring the fit.

"There, Brother Murray. Anyone would be honored to hire you in that jacket," Maddie's father said.

"This *is* my jacket." Murray beamed. "I guess it looked different because I hadn't seen it for so long."

Steve refrained from pointing out that Murray had stolen the jacket in the first place. The preacher would probably look on it as a deserved welcome gift from society.

Frank was becoming impatient. "We gotta go, Murr."

"Could I have a word with you?" Steve said pleasantly for the preacher's sake, but with a look that let Frank and Murray know he meant business. He indicated that they should step outside.

"Mr. Jackson, I trust you mean them no harm?"

"Daddy, they knocked Steve unconscious twice!" Maddie burst out.

Steve turned to face Maddie's father. "Sir, I don't know what they've told you, but I assure you I do not seek out violence." Preacher or not, he held the man's gaze until Preacher Givens looked away, then followed Murray and Frank outside onto the porch.

Steve skipped the social chitchat. "Last chance—is there anything in that jacket you want to tell me about?"

Frank grimaced. "Man, I keep tellin—"

"Save it." Steve cut him off. "The Gorilla's after that jacket because he thinks his missing doubloons are in it. They're not. So here's some free advice. Take the thing far away from here. Disappear. I'm only after the coins, and if you two don't have them, then you'll never see me again."

SO THIS WAS THE END.

Maddie hadn't expected it to be quite so abrupt, but now that Frank and Murray had the stupid jacket, there was no need for Steve to stay at Gloria's anymore.

Her father drove off with the two men, and Steve hoisted his duffel and followed Gloria and Maddie to her car.

"What will you do now?" she asked as her sister strapped Luke in his car seat. But the question she wanted to ask was, "Will I see you again?"

Unfortunately, she already knew the answer.

Steve squinted into the distance. "Go back to ground zero—the Green Bayou Hotel where the theft took place. I'll try to trace what happened to the jacket, take another look at the security videos and certainly talk with Murray's grandmother."

"If you need to look at the center's records, you know, so you can see the people we lent the jacket to before John took it home, I'll be glad to show them to you." *Too eager, Maddie.*

"Thanks. I may take you up on that." He looked into her eyes, his own dark and unreadable, then leaned down and gave her a quick kiss on the cheek. "'Bye, Maddie."

Maddie closed her eyes, wanting desperately to turn her head and have one final, real kiss, but Gloria was in the car watching them.

"Let me know what happens, okay?" *Callmecall-mecallme.*

"Sure." But she could tell he was only being polite.

He leaned in the car and spoke to Luke. "'Bye, little guy."

Think of a brilliant excuse to keep talking. Even an unbrilliant one. Something.

But she didn't. She watched him stride off and get on his motorcycle. Then pride forced her to get into the car before he saw her watch him drive off.

Besides, that's what rearview mirrors were for.

"He's a good man, Maddie," Gloria said after Maddie started the car.

"Steve?"

Gloria nodded.

"How do you know?" Maddie was truly curious.

"I can tell, can't you?"

Maddie backed down the driveway, avoiding the newly replanted pansies. "I *want* to think he's good—like you and Mom and Dad think everyone has goodness in them—but I don't have the knack for telling the difference between buried good and just plain bad."

"It's not a knack. You believe a person is good, and he'll try to live up to your faith in him."

"What if he doesn't?" Maddie was thinking of Doug the married scumbag.

"Sometimes good people choose to do things that aren't good," her sister replied.

So how do you know if it's a good person doing a bad thing, or a bad person doing a bad thing? Not to mention the bad people doing the occasional good things, probably by accident.

Maddie sighed. Every time she had one of these

conversations with her family, she ended up confused and frustrated. "Well, I thought Steve was a good man, too," she said finally. "Unfortunately, I'll never see him again."

STEVE HAD PROMISED Frank and Murray they'd never see him again, but that didn't mean he wasn't going to follow them.

Instead of returning to the center, Maddie's father drove them to the bus station—and probably gave them money for tickets—then drove off. Steve stayed behind and watched until Frank and Murray got on a Greyhound bus going north.

Smart move on their part. Maybe the first one ever.

And, according to his research, they hadn't been north since before the theft. Therefore, Steve could reasonably assume they were out of the coin hunt.

He exhaled and stretched his legs before getting back on his motorcycle and heading to the Lancaster.

There was a whirlpool tub he hadn't spent nearly enough time soaking in. The thought crossed his mind that it would be more fun soaking in it with Maddie.

A lot of things would be more fun with Maddie. Even arguing would be more fun with her. He smiled to himself, thinking of the humdingers they'd have, and then making up afterwards...

His smile faded. There would be no humdingers with Maddie—arguments or otherwise. He needed to move on.

He didn't want to. He just needed to.

THE REHEARSAL MAY or may not have gone off without a hitch. Maddie wasn't paying enough attention to tell. She was busy thinking about how she'd just let Steve ride out of her life. Not that she could have stopped him.

She supposed she could contact him if she tried really hard. She remembered the name of the insurance company he was working for on this job and if she wanted to humiliate herself, she could try leaving messages in all its branch offices.

But she knew he wouldn't call her back.

In the meantime, she shepherded her sheep, including Matthew, who had a tendency to boss the other lambs around. Maddie was inclined to let him. In fact, next year, she'd make him a sheepdog.

"Miss Maddie? I hafta go to the bathroom."

"Me, too," said another little voice.

"If Jason gets to go, then I do, too."

Matthew stood. "I can take them, Aunt Maddie."

"Shh." Maddie glanced over at her mother, serenely in control even though the rehearsal was running long and one of the three kings kept tripping over his robe.

Well, let her try to remain serene when faced with a dozen sheep with lamb-sized bladders. "Okay, we'll *all* go. Everybody remember to say 'baaa' as we leave the field."

As they baaed, Maddie got her purse and led her sheep out the side door. In this area of the center, the rest rooms were located in the hall behind the kitchen, which was closed for the evening.

Maddie dug in her purse for her keys and her hand closed over a plastic card with holes in it. Steve's room key from the Lancaster.

Maddie brought it out and stared at it.

"Aunt Maddie." Matthew jiggled her arm. "I think you'd better hurry."

Maddie found her keys and unlocked the doors. A flock of sheep stampeded inside. In the midst of it all, Maddie continued to stare at Steve's key. She really ought to return it.

In person.

Tonight.

MADDIE WAS NOT dressed for seduction, but she'd ditched the brown shepherd costume, and her all-weather coat covered up the fuzzy pink-headed reindeer sweater.

Now if she could only not be intimidated by the doorman. Maybe he wouldn't recognize her, since she wasn't carrying a crying baby this time.

Maddie breathed easier when she saw a different doorman standing out front. She gave her car keys to the valet, hoping that she wouldn't have to retrieve her car from the garage for a while.

As she walked through the glass doors on her way to the bank of elevators, Maddie considered lingering in the lobby until she knew what she was going to say to Steve.

She'd been so caught up in her own daring, that she hadn't dared to think much past this point.

Maddie hadn't had a lot of experience in the art of seduction—at least the woman's part—and recalled tidbits from the stories of wicked—but interesting—women she'd read about from the box of books donated to the center's library. A young, teenaged Maddie was supposed to sort and shelve the books and had stumbled across a series called, "Wicked Women of the World: Circumstances or Destiny?"

They were meant to be cautionary tales, but the only caution Maddie absorbed was to avoid accepting what life offered without trying to change what she didn't like.

She didn't like Steve leaving, therefore, she was creating the circumstances for her destiny.

If the elevator was destined to come before she lost her nerve.

At last it arrived and Maddie slipped inside. She tried not to hyperventilate and actually made it all the way to Steve's room before faltering.

She wasn't wicked and she wasn't a woman of the world, but she had a feeling her destiny was behind that door.

Maddie knocked.

Destiny didn't answer.

She listened, but didn't hear the television, or sounds of water running—so she put the key in the slot and turned the door handle.

What if he were asleep?

But he wasn't there. Maddie came on in, noting that there were a few personal items in the room, but Steve had obviously not returned since leaving Gloria's house earlier.

Maddie let out her breath. Now what?

Taking off her coat, she sat in a chair by the table, trying to look casual, but determined. After a few minutes, "casual and determined" became "tense and impatient."

It was too quiet in here. She turned on the TV and sat on the bed, but that was a little obvious. Not that the fact that she was in Steve's room at all wasn't plenty obvious enough. Or that she'd brought the canvas bag containing the clothes she'd had at Gloria's.

Maddie put the bag in the corner behind the chair. In doing so, she caught sight of herself in the mirror. The sweater had to go. She peeled it over her head, then had to deal with the static electricity in her hair.

Did the wicked women of the world ever deal with static electricity?

The white shirt she wore beneath the sweater now had bits of red fuzz on it. Maddie brushed and brushed at it, but it still looked pinkish. She unbuttoned the top two buttons to draw Steve's attention away from her sartorial inadequacies, but he was hardly a two-button kind of guy. Maddie unbuttoned a third button, but now her shirt looked like it had come unbuttoned by accident.

She sighed. She couldn't even dress to thrill. She rebuttoned the button. Why hadn't she planned this better?

Because this was the perfect opportunity—her only opportunity. Her parents would think she was at Gloria's. Gloria would think she was at the center with her parents.

Walking over to the full-length mirror on the closet door, Maddie studied herself with an eye toward making improvements, no matter how slight.

The jeans weren't bad, but the tennies had to go. She took them off and got the bright idea of getting back on the bed to watch TV. A person would take off her shoes if she was going to lie on a bed and watch TV. Maddie would look like she'd just casually made herself at home while she waited for him. No biggie. Approachable without being too obvious.

But what was she going to say when he walked through the door?

She ought to rehearse this.

Maddie positioned the closet door so that she could see herself on the bed. She decided to lay on her stomach facing the foot of the bed and the TV. Casual. Approachable.

Steve would come in the door, she'd turn her head, and...

"Hi." Soft and welcoming.

The TV was too loud for soft and welcoming. Maddie turned it down. And what was this? The local news? *That* was real romantic. She flipped through the channels until she found an innocuous rerun.

Now, one more time. She turned her head to the door and smiled. "Hi!" Too perky.

Again. "Hi." Too throaty.

And again. "Hello." Too telephony.

Maddie dropped her head and moaned into the comforter. Okay. She'd try to imagine Steve's point of view as he walked through the door, thinking he was coming back to an empty room and finding Maddie lounging on his bed.

"Maddie!" he'd exclaim in delighted surprise. "Oh, my darling, I'd hoped against hope that you would come to me. I've been such a fool. You're the perfect woman for me. My life will be empty without you. I know an all-night chapel..."

Uh-huh. Right.

Besides, that would mean she'd get married in jeans and a pink-headed reindeer sweater.

Besides...marriage. Talk about delusional. Steve wasn't going to be thinking marriage, even if Maddie... She'd lost her mind. She'd completely lost her mind.

And her heart, too, it would appear.

It was time to take a look at her goals, here. The wicked women always had known what they wanted. What exactly did Maddie want?

Steve.

She was going to have to be more specific.

Steve. Forever and ever.

And more realistic.

Steve—for a really great night?

Better.

Steve—who after a really great night wanted more really great nights?

And then what? Maddie sat up and punched the TV remote.

What destiny was she trying to seize?

Steve's. Then *he* could be in charge.

She shook her head. Women of the world, wicked or not, were supposed to be in charge of their own destinies. It was just that she liked his better than hers.

So change yours.

Could she?

Working with Steve had felt right in a way that working with her family never had. *Being* with him had felt right in a way that being with her family never had. She didn't have to watch what she said, or how she said it around him.

He seemed to accept her for who she was and not who she should be.

How could she give that up?

She couldn't.

The realization made her shiver. That was it. She wanted to go with Steve. On his terms.

However, when he walked in the door, she couldn't just jump up and say, "Take me with you!"

Which brought her back full circle to her rehearsing.

"Hi. We need to talk." Oh, ick. Men hated that one.

"Hi. I didn't feel we had a chance to say a proper goodbye so I came here..." A Victorian-sounding variation on the we-need-to-talk theme.

She could take off all her clothes and get in bed, and then she wouldn't have to say anything.

The closer to midnight it got, the better that option looked. The innocuous rerun on TV was over and so was the next one, and Steve still hadn't returned.

It was late, and Maddie was worried. She turned off the TV and paced, and not even her luxurious surroundings distracted her.

What if Steve had been hurt? What if he'd crashed his motorcycle and was in a hospital somewhere? What if—

The door handle turned.

Maddie froze. Steve stepped into the room, saw her standing there, and stopped.

They stared at each other.

He seemed to be in one piece—and what a piece it was. "Where have you been?" she blurted.

"Maddie?" After his initial surprise, Steve

dropped his duffel and strode over to her. "What's happened? Is everybody all right?"

"No, I'm not all right! I was worried about you. I kept imagining all sorts of horrible—"

"Maddie," he interrupted her gently, his hands on her arms. "What are you doing here?"

She drew a shuddering breath. Great. Two hours of rehearsal down the drain. "I, uh, found your key when I was taking the sheep to the bathroom."

That wasn't on her mental script either. What a time to ad-lib.

A corner of his mouth quivered, but he didn't break out into a smile. Maddie could have used a smile right then. "You could've left the key at the front desk."

Not very encouraging. Maddie nodded. "I know."

"But you didn't."

"No, I didn't."

He raised his eyebrows, clearly waiting for an explanation.

Which meant she had to give him one. "I wanted to see you. We...we said goodbye so fast, and after all we'd been through I didn't feel..." How was it possible for him to have grown even more good looking since she'd seen him last?

His arms slid away. "Didn't feel...?"

She'd had two hours to think of something to say. Why hadn't she? "It didn't seem...enough, so I thought..." If he'd just kiss her senseless, then she wouldn't have to worry about finishing a sentence.

"You thought...?"

She inhaled deeply. "That I'd seduce you."

He blinked.

Maddie blinked back. "I'm not doing a very good job, am I?"

"You'd be surprised." He turned away, snagged his duffel from in front of the door and put it in the closet. Removing his leather coat, he hung it up, then shut the mirrored doors. Each movement was very deliberate, as though he was thinking, or angry, or both.

He took two steps into the room, drew his hands to his waist and looked at her. "I'm leaving tomorrow morning."

It was what she'd suspected. "I know. That's why I'm here now."

"You spending the night here won't change anything."

"So you've said. Repeatedly. You want me to sign a liability release form?"

Maddie couldn't read the expression on his face. It wasn't pleased, but he hadn't thrown her out yet, either. If he'd just raise his arms, she'd run into them and all would be well.

But he didn't.

Maddie lifted her chin as though by doing so, she could prevent more of her self-confidence from evaporating.

"I'm going to take a shower," he said at last. "A long, hot shower. Not a cold one."

"You want me to join you?"

He closed his eyes. "No. Yes, but no." He looked at her again. "When I'm in the shower, take the time to consider what you're doing."

"I've been considering it for the last two hours!"

"Maddie, you're a white-picket-fence kind of girl

and I'm a free-range kind of guy. Have you considered that? Or have you painted a pretty little hearts-and-flowers picture of the way you'd like things to be?"

"Of course, I have. But I also know it's as unrealistic as the bleak picture you've painted. You're not the blackhearted...cad, for the lack of a better word, that you think you are."

"Oh, I am, Maddie. I am. Don't believe that because I'm giving you this opportunity to change your mind and walk out of here that I have even one drop of goodness in me."

"Yes, you do."

"I don't *want* to be good and if you're headed in that direction, you go alone."

"Why *wouldn't* you want to be good?"

"To be good, you have to not mind people taking advantage of you. I resent it like hell. And I can't forgive—at least not until I've gotten even."

"That's not the real reason."

He stared hard at her, his jaw working, before he looked away.

"No," he confirmed, speaking with a quiet finality. "My old man had a black temper and I've got it, too."

When he looked back at her, his expression was defiant which Maddie knew wasn't anything more than Steve covering up an ancient hurt.

She remembered him telling Luke about his childhood, remembered trying not to sob aloud. "You are not your father. And even if you did inherit his temper, you've learned how to handle it."

"I handle it by keeping to myself. Some men aren't

meant to be domesticated, Maddie. So if you stay, I'll take what you're offering and give nothing back. And I'll enjoy it."

"Are you telling me you're a selfish lover?"

"On the contrary." The smile he gave her was pure, masculine self-confidence. "You'll have a good time, but when it's over, baby, it's over."

11

M AYBE FOR HIM it would be.

And Maddie wasn't even sure she believed that. There was something in his eyes, something that told her he was trying to scare her away, but hoping she didn't scare all that easily.

"Fine," she said. "But, buster, you better make it one hell of a good time."

She didn't normally swear and hoped she pulled it off.

By the way Steve's eyes narrowed, she couldn't exactly tell, so she gazed back at him and tried to look like a wicked woman of the world. He'd named his terms, and she'd decided to accept them.

He unbuckled his belt. "No strings is fine with you?"

"Been there, done that."

"Not by choice," he said dryly, then slowly slithered the black leather belt through the loops of his jeans.

"So now it's my choice." Maddie tried to maintain eye contact and not watch the belt's progress.

"Is it?" Steve dropped the belt and brought his hands back to his waist.

Maddie swallowed. Maybe she should be doing that. Except she wasn't wearing a belt. Or maybe she should be undressing *him.* Except now he wasn't wearing a belt, either.

If he could give her a sign, or something, instead of just watching her.

A few more moments of the unnerving silence ticked by, then Steve grabbed the waist of his T-shirt and jerked it over his head all in one devastatingly smooth movement.

Maddie flinched—it was the suddenness, she told herself. Not to mention being hit with the visual confirmation of Steve's genuine hunk status. Talk about a sign.

She'd been held against that chest before, but seeing the muscles defined in all their glory, covered with the perfect amount of dark hair, well, it made her weak. That's why her knees wouldn't work. She had no choice but to stand there and stare at him. Any woman would have, she told herself.

This was a lot of man. More than all the men in Maddie's life put together.

In fact, Maddie felt sorry for other men. She was now spoiled for them. They could never measure up.

Balling the shirt into a wad, Steve tossed it over his shoulder and stalked toward her.

A lot of man was coming her way. Instinctively, Maddie backed up and felt the bed touch her calves. She scrambled to remain upright, but a second later found herself unseductively bouncing on the mattress. Maybe he'd think she was being playful.

Steve loomed over her. Maddie wished he wouldn't loom.

He swooped down—which Maddie wished he wouldn't do, either. She fell back onto her elbows and he planted a hand on either side of her, bringing his face close to hers.

Maddie braced herself and stared into eyes so brown they were nearly black. Eyes which gazed deeply into hers.

"You're not ready," Steve said with a gruff tenderness. "But I'm flattered, Maddie."

Then he brushed his lips across her forehead—like...like she was a child, pushed himself off the bed and walked toward the bathroom, closing the door before Maddie regained her power of speech.

And the only reason she'd lost her power of speech was because the view of his back was just as good as his front, she told herself.

Then she told herself to get real. He was right. She *hadn't* been ready.

But she was now.

BEHIND THE BATHROOM door, Steve turned on the shower, then stared at the door. He hoped he hadn't made her cry. The thought of Maddie in tears was almost enough to send him back into the bedroom. But it was better for her to cry now, because if she stuck around with him, she'd be crying later for sure.

Finding her here tonight, after he'd been thinking about her, had been like getting kicked in the head. Saying goodbye to her once had been hard enough, but twice? It was more than a man should be expected to do. Steve glanced at himself in the mirror, just checking to see if he had a halo.

There wasn't one, but from his point of view, there should have been.

Maddie was...Maddie. It was the combination of

savviness and innocence that got to him. If she were all one and not the other, she wouldn't nearly as appealing.

She'd actually thought she could spend the night with him before he left in the morning. If he'd agreed, he'd have destroyed the innocent part of her, the part that believed in a goodness that wasn't there. And when she found out he was exactly as he said he was, she wouldn't be Maddie anymore.

He couldn't bear that thought.

He knew what she was thinking. It all went back to the C's not mixing with the T's. Maddie thought she could try temporary, just the way Steve had thought he could try commitment. It hadn't worked for him, and it wasn't going to work for her. The next step was to hope temporary became permanent. It was logical when you wanted to be with somebody.

But Steve had seen her family. He'd had the glimpse into her life. He *could—not—live* that way. Not even for her. So he was going to stand in that shower for as long as it took to wash away the thought of her.

THE SOUND OF THE water running jolted all awkwardness and hesitancy from Maddie. She relaxed and warmth returned to her fingers and toes. To her heart, too.

What a great, big, misguided sweetie he was. He was trying to save her from herself. And it was so endearingly obvious that he hadn't had any experience saving women from themselves, otherwise he'd know that taking off his shirt wasn't the way to do it.

Steve thought she was going to run out the room,

thankful for her great escape. Nope. Maddie had a new goal: seeing him naked.

So it was a short-term goal. She didn't care.

Once she'd accomplished that goal, she could move on to other goals involving nakedness and touching and kissing, in no particular order.

She needed to do a little stage setting. Maddie picked up Steve's belt and shirt and hung them up, then turned off the room lights except for the floor lamp in the corner by the drapes. The room was still too bright for the subdued effect she wanted, so she unscrewed one of the light bulbs. There. Interesting shadows at the edges, but everything was visible.

The shower was still running. Maddie turned down the covers on the bed, then removed the drugstore sack from her purse. Wicked women of the world were prepared.

Which side of the bed to put the box? Or should she put it in one of the drawers? Compromising, Maddie opened the box and put a couple of packets in each drawer and one by the telephone. That would be Steve's side, she determined, not that she planned to let him sleep a whole lot. After all, she was only counting on one night.

All righty, then. Maddie looked around the room, wondering if she dared order something from room service, and decided that would be pushing her luck. Besides, there was always the mini bar. So that only left her attire. The huge oversized T-shirt she'd slept in at Gloria's wasn't her first choice. However, if she wore one of *Steve's* shirts...

With an ear out for the shower, Maddie took off her clothes and hung them in the closet, right by

Steve's. She took his black T-shirt and slipped it on, but it was too short. Interesting effect—maybe for breakfast, which, if she wore the black T-shirt, might become brunch.

There was the blue denim one he'd worn the other day, but Maddie finally just chose to put on the hotel's terry-cloth robe and wait.

And wait.

And pace.

The water continued to run. What was he *doing* in there?

STEVE PROPPED HIS hands against the tile and let the water beat on his back.

His fingers were shriveling, his skin was pink, and Maddie was gone by now.

Gone. Out of his life.

So this was how being good felt. No wonder he didn't like it.

MADDIE ARRANGED HERSELF on the bed, loosely tying the belt of the robe, letting her legs show. She'd tousled her hair so it would look...tousled, she supposed. Just something other than the neatly parted, tucked-behind-the-ears look she normally wore.

She was ready.

The shower continued to run.

After a while, Maddie rolled onto her back. She refused to turn on the television and wasn't keen on the radio, either. Maybe she should read something. Scooting off the bed, she went over to the desk and found the room-service menu, a magazine touting the wonders of Houston and a television guide.

Some papers of Steve's were there, as well, but Maddie didn't look at them.

Sighing, she took the Houston tourist magazine and went back to the bed. Propping her head on her fist, she flipped through the ads for restaurants she'd never eaten in and studied the models dressed in clothes she knew she'd see in the thrift shop a couple of years down the road.

Her eyelids grew heavy. She must have dozed for a second because her elbow slipped and knocked the magazine onto the floor, waking her in the process. Great. Maddie crept forward on her stomach and reached down. As her fingers touched glossy paper, she became aware of the silence.

Steve had finished his shower!

A split second later, the bathroom door opened, catching her hanging off the edge of the bed.

She looked up, caught the full force of bare chest and low riding towel, then slipped and slid the rest of the way off the bed landing next to a pair of wrinkled male feet.

"Maddie?" Steve's voice was barely above a whisper.

"What?" she snapped.

"I didn't think you'd be here."

I can still salvage this. Standing, she tightened the sash of the robe and pushed back her now genuinely tousled hair. "Well, I *am* here."

Then she met his eyes. They were dark, not with passion, but with pain.

"What have I done to you?" He sounded so serious.

"Nothing yet. I'm hoping you'll fix that."

He looked at her sternly. "Are you prepared for—"

"Oh, I sprinkled preparation all over the room."

"I meant emotionally, but it's good to know about the other, too."

Be daring. Be bold. Maddie stepped forward and touched his chest with both hands, spanning them outward before burying her fingers in the slightly damp curls.

He didn't move, but she felt his heartbeat quicken.

She looked up at his face and saw that he was gritting his teeth, so she stood on tiptoe and kissed his jaw. Or near it. He was taller than she was and wasn't giving her any help.

Fine, then. She'd just make do with the glorious hunk of male chest right at eye level. She leaned forward inhaling the fresh soapy smell and pressed her lips just a little left of center, right over his heart.

The breath hissed between his teeth and in the next instant Maddie felt herself caught up in his arms, Scarlett O'Hara-style.

Steve slowly walked forward until he reached the edge of the bed. The sash on the robe had loosened and Maddie felt the lapels pull apart. She let them and watched Steve's gaze dip to her throat. Winding her arms around his neck, she brought his face to hers.

He met her more than halfway. Almost as soon as his lips touched hers, he crushed her against him, kissing her with a deep thoroughness that made her glad he was holding her, because she knew she wouldn't have been able to stand on her own.

It was a demanding as well as challenging kiss, full of passion and revealing the scope of his desire.

Maddie not only met the challenge, she made a few demands of her own, eliciting a deep groan from him.

He wrenched himself away and set her on the bed. "This isn't like you," he said, and Maddie was pleased to hear his rough breathing. "And it's my fault."

"But it *is* me! The other me wasn't me. I wasn't happy and I was trying so hard to be...and then I met you."

He looked down on her with exasperated tenderness. "Have you ever thought that you're using my bad influence on you as an excuse?"

"You mean so I won't have to take responsibility for my actions?"

"Yeah."

"No."

"Think about it now."

Maddie sat and looked at her clasped hands. "Thought about it. Don't care."

"Maddie, I've corrupted you. I'm bad for you."

"Is that why I want you bad?"

"*Maddie.*"

"You know, if you want to continue playing cheap pop psychologist as foreplay—which I've gotta tell you isn't doing it for me—then it's my turn. *I* say you and your kisses are trying to seduce me into seducing *you* so you don't have to feel guilty."

He looked flummoxed.

"See? See? Caught you, didn't I?"

"No...I don't know. I can't figure out what you meant."

She spoke slowly. "If I'm on the offense and you put up a token, paltry, tissue paper defense, then you can satisfy the I-did-the-right-thing button on your man-o-meter."

"My *man-o-meter*?"

"Yeah." Reaching out, Maddie gave the slightest tug to the knot on his towel. That was all it took for the towel to open and fall to the floor. She blinked. "Well, ding ding ding."

The slow grin he gave her was the sweetest she'd ever seen. It was a combination of masculine pride, and yes, love. Maddie knew they weren't using the "l" word, but it was there in his eyes.

As she knew it was in hers.

"Maddie, what am I going to do with you?"

"I've got a few ideas."

"Ideas, I've got." He slid into the bed until he was behind her.

Maddie tried to turn around but he caught her around the waist and pulled her to him until she was firmly nestled against his chest, captured between two rock-hard thighs.

"I can't see you," she protested, but not too much.

"Close your eyes and feel."

That she could do.

As he spoke, Steve pulled her hair away from the side of her neck and gently kissed behind her ear. While Maddie dealt with an immediate and severe case of goose bumps, he reached in front of her with both hands and slowly untied the robe's sash.

Her heart pounded. Her throat was dry. Prickles chased each other across her skin.

Steve moved his hands to her neck and pulled the heavy terry-cloth lapels apart and off her shoulders. He drew them down her arms, moving slowly, but surely, kissing each sliver of skin as it was revealed. About halfway down her arms, the weight of the robe caused it to drop to her waist.

Steve unhurriedly drew each of her arms through the sleeves. "I love women's backs," he murmured. "I enjoy looking at them almost as much as I enjoy kissing them. You have a beautiful back, Maddie."

No man had ever told Maddie she had a beautiful back. No man had ever paid much attention to it before. Maddie found that her back liked having attention paid to it—a lot.

At least the kind of attention Steve paid. With his hands on her shoulders, thumbs lightly kneading the muscles at the base of her neck, he kissed his way down her spine drawing sensuous circles with his tongue.

There were nerves in her back. Who knew?

Maddie wanted to touch him—she ached to touch him. She ran her hands up and down his thighs and over his knees. His legs were strong and had well-defined muscles. Great legs, but they were legs all the same. She made a tiny sound of frustration.

"Patience, Maddie," Steve murmured next to her ear, then nipped it, making her gasp.

"Patience has never been one of my strengths." She tried to twist, but he held her fast. "Steve!"

He chuckled, then ran his hands down her sides until they spanned her waist. The whole time, his mouth and tongue worked their magic at her neck and then along the underside of her jaw. Maddie leaned back and turned her head as far as it would go until she could meet his lips with hers.

She felt his smile as he kissed her mouth with the same maddeningly gentle pressure he'd been using on her back. Maddie leaned into the kiss, but Steve moved away maintaining the same pressure. Sighing, she broke the kiss.

"Ah, my sweet Maddie," he breathed into her ear, his breath sensitizing the nerves in her neck.

He drew her closer to him, so that his chest pressed against her back, then slowly brought his hands around to her stomach. His fingers fanned outward, touching the delicate skin of her inner thighs before moving upward toward her ribs.

Maddie's heart threatened to beat its way out of her chest. Involuntarily, she arched her back. Involuntarily, because she liked feeling the soft hair of his chest against her and didn't want to move away—but his hands' leisurely journey was driving her nuts. Each nerve in her skin telegraphed the location to the next along the path, so by the time Steve actually caressed her, it was like being touched twice.

When his hands finally closed over her breasts, Maddie bit her lip to keep from crying out, gave up and cried out anyway.

The relief was short-lived before the sweet agony began to build again.

"I can't stand this!" she moaned, moving restlessly.

"Maddie, I'm just getting warmed up."

"I'm hot enough for both of us." She dropped her

head back against his shoulder, nearly weeping in frustration.

Just when she thought she couldn't stand any more, he released his hold, turning her in his arms.

Maddie was all for that. She flipped over to her knees and practically launched herself at him sending them both tumbling onto the pillows.

He laughed, his chest vibrating against her chin. She laughed too, then pressed dozens of frantic kisses across his stomach, chest and in the hollow of his throat.

She was too impatient to play his tortuous game. She wanted him too much. How could he stand it?

But maybe he couldn't. His hands had stilled and his eyes were closed. His breathing sounded labored. All signs that he wasn't as in control as he wanted her to believe.

Maddie liked the idea of Steve being a little out of control. Freeing her hands from between them, she planted one on either side of him and inched her way up his body, until they were pressed fully against each other. Maddie took a moment to press her ear against his chest and listen to the thudding of his heart, then moved until they were nose to nose, chin to chin, and mouth to mouth.

She drew back until he opened his eyes. Then she smiled and kissed him, boldly thrusting her tongue into his mouth until he shuddered.

HE WAS LOST AND he knew it. But did she know it?

At that moment, Maddie gave him a knowing look

as womanly as he'd ever seen from her and kissed him.

She knew it.

Steve shuddered, knowing he was now vulnerable. Maddie stroked the inside of his mouth in a suggestive rhythm that nearly brought his blood to a boil.

He clutched at her and desperately tried to slow her down. This was supposed to be *her* evening. He was supposed to be making love to *her*. He didn't want to find fulfillment with Maddie Givens. It seemed purer, somehow, if he didn't. A punishment for leaving her, he guessed.

But Maddie was inflicting her own brand of punishment. When he seized her hips, she pressed her torso seductively against him.

And her kisses...what had he taught her and what had she improvised on her own?

In a moment, it didn't matter.

In a moment, nothing would matter except becoming as close to Maddie as he could.

He swept his hands from her hips, across her magnificent back, and buried his fingers in her hair, holding her to him, afraid she'd stop.

And then she did stop, determinedly pulling her mouth away.

"*Maddie.*" Her name was torn from him.

"What? You only like to drive people insane with lust—you don't like a little lust insanity for yourself?" She looked entirely too pleased with herself.

Steve supposed it wasn't fair to draw on his training to flip her over on her back, and straddle her, but that's what he did.

Instead of realizing how serious the situation she'd created was, Maddie giggled and reached downward, closing her hand around him.

Steve countered by closing his mouth over her breast, though as a counter strategy, it proved useless.

Still, her sharply drawn breath proved she wasn't as fully in the dominant position as she thought.

She tugged at him insistently.

"Not yet," he managed to say.

"Yes, yet."

Steve managed to capture both her hands and hold them above her head.

"Steve!"

"Okay, Maddie. This is for you." He recaptured her breast with his mouth while his free hand sought the juncture of her thighs.

Turning her head from side to side, she moaned and it was the sweetest sound Steve had ever heard.

"Come on, Maddie," he urged her.

"No...I want you with me..." Her breath came in panting gasps.

"It'll be better for you this way," he soothed.

"I know what I want!" she snarled.

Surprise made him loosen his grip on her wrists. She freed her hands, fumbled around near the telephone and threw something at him. "Put it on— now!"

He liked being ordered around by her. "Yes ma'am." He went for the packet, ripped it open, and stopped.

She whimpered. "Please hurry."

Steve's hand shook. For a split second, he'd felt regret—regret because out of nowhere he'd felt a primal urge to plant a baby—his child—in Maddie. He wanted her to be its mother and he'd never felt that way with any woman.

But hadn't he known Maddie wasn't just any woman?

"Steve!"

He fumbled a second more, then leaned over her. "I'm here, sweet Maddie."

A moment later, guided by her urging hands, he entered her.

They stilled.

"Oh, thank you," Maddie whispered, and wrapped her legs around him.

He should be thanking *her*. Steve felt an unfamiliar stinging behind his eyes as he thrust deeply within her, determined to give her as much pleasure as he could.

But this was Maddie and he lost himself in her, forgetting to hold back until her shudders prompted his own release.

Afterwards, he held her silently, afraid he'd say something he shouldn't or make promises he couldn't keep.

Maddie didn't seem to notice and fell asleep after kissing him gently.

Steve didn't sleep at all the rest of the night. He thought long and hard about his life, the kind of man he was, and the kind of man Maddie deserved.

He wasn't that man.

In the predawn, he slipped from her embrace and packed his things, then returned to the bed, thinking only to spend a few more minutes watching Maddie sleep.

"Have a good life, Maddie. Find some guy and have babies. Be happy." He brushed the hair from her forehead and brushed his lips across it.

When he pulled back, her eyes fluttered open. "Oh, good. You're awake." She held out her arms.

It would take a stronger man than Steve to walk away right then.

This time, his lovemaking was gentle and bitter-sweet, but no less earth-shattering. He also dozed afterwards, awakening later, but still before Maddie.

And this time, he walked out the door.

12

MADDIE COULDN'T believe he'd actually gone. No note. No anything. Yes, he'd said he'd leave, but after what they'd shared, how could he?

He'd warned her. He'd been very clear. He'd given her the chance to leave.

And still, Maddie had thought he'd stay.

She'd told him she was emotionally prepared and at the time she thought she was. She wasn't.

Once again, Maddie had given her heart, her body, and this time her soul, to a man who didn't want them.

HE'D FORSAKEN HIS motorcycle for a nondescript rental car. For three days, Steve had traced the doubloons and all trails led back to the center. Perversely, this made him happy, because for three nights, he'd returned, himself, hoping to see Maddie.

Hoping she wouldn't see him.

Sometimes, he'd catch a glimpse of her in the serving line at the soup kitchen, but it wasn't nearly enough.

But today was Christmas Eve, and he knew she'd be here for the pageant, so he was, too.

He'd been sitting in the parked car for an hour, going quietly mad from the blinking lights and *Feliz*

Navidad blaring from Casa Garcia, and yet he wasn't going to leave without seeing Maddie.

He had it bad. That's when he finally admitted he'd broken his most important personal rule—he'd fallen in love with her.

The admission brought no relief. He couldn't do anything about it except go through life more miserable than he already was. In another week, he'd call this case quits—which was probably a week longer than he should spend on it.

The doubloons were long gone, either thrown out, lost, or with someone who was content to hide them away. He was just hanging around Houston because he wanted to see Maddie.

People were gathering for the pageant. He'd seen at least three lambs and two angels hopping and skipping inside. And then he'd seen Maddie's car arrive and park down the street. She was dressed in a brown costume, different from the first one he'd seen her in. He watched as she walked along the sidewalk, holding the rough material around her.

She should be wearing a coat, Steve thought. She didn't take care of herself the way she should. He watched until she'd gone inside, and even then, waited in case she'd forgotten something in her car.

He almost didn't see them. He was concentrating on the main entrance to the center and wasn't paying attention to the soup kitchen and thrift shop.

The two men who approached had coats on—nice ones. Suits and ties, as well, if Steve didn't miss his guess.

Sunday shoes. Feeling that prickle that he'd learned to trust, Steve got out a pair of small night-vision binoculars, and stared at the men's feet. They were wearing black leather that gleamed in the streetlight with a professional shine. Sunday shoes.

These were Cortavilla's men. He was as certain as if they'd carried signs announcing the fact.

Why were they here now? Because it was Christmas Eve and people would be distracted, Steve answered his own question. Getting out of the car as quietly as he could, he walked half a block up the street to the gas station on the corner and shoved his com card into the phone.

So far, the men hadn't committed a crime, but Steve figured breaking and entering was only moments away.

They must be desperate to take the chance, and desperate thugs were even more dangerous than normal. Steve figured they'd been given an ultimatum and more than their jobs was on the line.

Maddie and her family and a lot of other innocent people were in there. Who knew what these guys had in mind?

Steve could picture Maddie challenging the men and experienced a wave of nausea worse than the first time he'd crossed the open sea in a crew boat.

He asked for his contact with the Houston Police Department, and then with the FBI, but it was Christmas Eve. There was a skeleton staff. The men were with their families, etcetera, etcetera. Steve didn't bother to listen to the rest. He interrupted the dispatcher with the instructions to send the most senior detective on duty and back up units, gave her a code number, then disconnected the call and removed his card.

They'd want verification, and Steve didn't want to take the time. He hoped the dispatcher on duty tonight wasn't a stickler for protocol.

IT WAS CHRISTMAS EVE, and Maddie wasn't in the spirit. The pageant was tonight and she wanted to be anywhere but in the middle of a group of excited five-year-old sheep.

Her family glowed with inner light and tranquility. Maddie felt dead inside.

No one seemed to notice that anything was wrong. Gloria and her parents obviously hadn't talked about her to the point of figuring out that Maddie'd spent the night with neither of them three nights ago.

That night had changed her, devastated her on one level, to be sure, but Steve's legacy wasn't all bad. How could it be when she loved him?

After much thought, Maddie had decided to resign from her teaching job. She didn't even want to finish out the school year, but she would keep teaching until they found a replacement. As soon as that happened, Maddie intended to find a full-time job doing something else. She knew the job she wanted, but since she couldn't have it, maybe there would be something similar.

A full-time job would preclude her working at the center except on weekends, which was what she wanted. Too, she wanted to earn enough money to rent her own apartment in spite of her parents insisting it was a waste. Maddie may not have been able to go with Steve, but that didn't mean she could stay here as though nothing had changed.

Everything had changed. Instead of helping her

family live the kind of lives they wanted, Maddie intended to live the life *she* wanted.

Maddie sat on a folding chair in the back of the rec room with Luke as Gloria and her mother made last-minute set and costume repairs with the glue gun. For some reason, Luke was fussy and it only reminded Maddie of the way Steve's voice could calm him down.

But since Steve wasn't here, she thought with bitter resignation, Luke would have to make due with sock puppets.

She pulled out one from the diaper bag. "Hey Luke, it's me, Harry Yellow Eyes." She spoke in a low voice, hoping to imitate Steve.

Luke wasn't buying it, or Harry Yellow Eyes. She tried the other one she rechristened Steve the Snake, but that wasn't fair. He'd done exactly as he'd said he'd do. She'd wanted one night—one great night—and that's exactly what she'd gotten, along with an early-morning bonus.

Luke didn't like Steve the Snake, either. Maddie put the sock puppets away, slung the diaper bag over her shoulder and tried pacing with Luke.

The rec room was filling, mostly with parents who'd had to bring their children early.

Gloria was still busy, so Maddie took Luke and went to the room where the sheep and angels were assembling. She'd left Matt in charge of the sheep, but it was still early enough that only two other lambs were there.

"Aunt Maddie, I think we should all have a rest room break before the play," he said.

"Good idea," Maddie replied, "Would you like to take yours now to save time?"

He nodded, and smothering her smile, Maddie signaled the woman in charge of the angels that she was leaving, and opened the hall door leading to the rest rooms.

It might not be a bad time to change Luke, either. Maybe that's why he was so fussy.

Passing by the dark kitchen, Maddie automatically looked through the windows, seeing the light from the hall reflected on the other side. It wasn't until she was bringing Matt and Luke back and looked again that she realized something wasn't right about the light. Where was her silhouette?

A split second later, she figured out that she was seeing the light on in the thrift shop. But the thrift shop was closed and her family had a thing about wasting electricity and thus the natural resources of the earth, so Maddie knew the lights had been turned off. Which meant—

"Maddie!"

She blinked at the dark figure coming toward her. "Steve?" For one incredulous moment, her heart leaped, the birds chirped, the sky was filled with rainbows, and a heavenly chorus sang in glorious four-part harmony.

Steve had come back for her.

"Hi, Mr. Steve!" Matt said. "Have you come to see our play?"

"Maybe, Matt," he said, but he was clearly caught off guard.

He hadn't come back for her. Maddie's heart returned to normal and the special effects switched off.

"Shouldn't you be taking your place?" Steve asked the little boy.

"Go on ahead, Matt," Maddie told him. "I'll be right there."

Matt looked like he wanted to argue, but Maddie held the door open for him. As soon as he'd walked through it, she turned to a grim-faced Steve.

"What is it?"

"Maddie, someone has broken into your thrift shop."

She nodded, shifting Luke to her other shoulder, hoping Steve would take him and soothe him. Maybe soothe her, too, while he was at it. "I saw the light." In more ways than one.

"I've already called the police, but it wouldn't hurt for you to do so, as well."

"Guess where the nearest phone is?" She nodded toward the thrift shop. "I'll have to run upstairs and use our line. Could you hold Luke for me? He's fussy tonight."

Proud of herself for thinking clearly and decisively and not shouting "How could you's" at Steve, Maddie ran up the stairs and reported the break-in.

When she returned, it was to find Steve pacing at the back of the rec room.

"The police are already sending somebody," Maddie told him.

He nodded tersely and handed her back Luke, all the while avoiding looking at her.

"I'm not going to cause a scene, if that's what's bothering you," she said.

He gave her a half smile. "I was afraid I might."

His eyes roamed over her, bringing memories of the other night back into sharp focus.

But Maddie wouldn't smile back. "I thought you were leaving town."

"I'm doing just what I said I'd do. I went back to the Green Bayou Hotel, and I talked with Murray's grandmother. All paths for the doubloons eventually lead right back here. I'm guessing Cortavilla's men have reached the same conclusion."

"You think they're the ones in the thrift shop?"

He started to nod, but stopped, looking over Maddie's shoulder. "No. I think they're the ones standing in the doorway."

Maddie literally felt her blood run cold. "What should I do?" Maddie didn't dare turn around and look. Suddenly all the happy Christmas pageant preparations took on a sinister perspective.

"Try ignoring them. Maybe they'll go away when they see it's obvious that no one here has lots of money."

"Come in, friends," sounded a voice. Maddie's father.

Steve whispered a word that would have been worth five dollars in the cuss can.

Maddie looked and saw her father ushering in two men in black all-weather coats and plaid scarves. "You're a little early. The pageant will start at seven-thirty. You're welcome to sit here and join in the pre-program caroling which is getting ready to start."

"You the guy who runs the place?" asked one man with a slight accent.

"I'm Preacher Givens, yes."

"We want to talk to you about something of ours that's gone missing."

Maddie listened to the conversation with a rapidly growing panic. "Steve, do something!"

He was already approaching the men. "Preacher Givens, I understand you're needed back with the lambs and angels."

Maddie's father gave Steve a cool look. "After I have a word with these gentlemen."

In the doorway behind the men, Maddie could see red and blue lights flashing and reflecting off the windows.

Her father saw the lights, too. "Why, whatever is the matter out there?"

The two men looked behind them and down the hall, then took off running across the room, pushing people and chairs out of their way. And right behind them ran Steve.

One chair careened into the pole supporting the stable, causing the grass roof to collapse on that side. There were a few startled screams, but within seconds, Gloria had gone to the piano and began playing "Joy to the World." Maddie's parents signaled that everyone should join in the singing and the panic was averted.

Maddie made her way to the main entrance as quickly as she could. In spite of the caroling, other concerned people crowded behind her as she stood at the door.

Be careful, Steve.

She remembered him saying that he left the apprehension of crooks to the authorities, so why was he chasing the men now?

He ran faster than they did, but not as fast as the police cruiser that cut off their escape.

The two men plowed into the side of the car. Steve grabbed one man as the door opened and the officer stopped the other.

The whole time, Maddie's heart beat so fast she couldn't feel where one thump ended and another began. If something happened to him...

But nothing did. It was all over in a few minutes that seemed longer than they actually were.

Maddie expected Steve to leave once the excitement was over, and had steeled herself for nothing more than a quick goodbye when he returned during the set repairs.

"Is everybody okay?" he asked.

She nodded. "And you?"

"Yeah."

They stared at each other, then Maddie looked away.

"It'll be a Merry Christmas for the Houston Police," Steve said. "They've been trying to get their hands on those two for some time. Now they owe me and they're inclined to be generous with their resources since I'm still looking for those doubloons." He didn't look as pleased as Maddie thought he would.

She had to ask. "Does that mean you're staying for a while?"

His eyes burned into hers. "Maddie, I can't. Nothing's changed." He looked around, then led her into a hallway.

"Look, I...care for you," he said.

"Care?" She let scorn color her voice.

He had the grace to look embarrassed. "It doesn't matter what I feel now. I know that eventually...Maddie..." His face looked drawn. "I almost hit my wife, just the way my dad hit my mom. One day, I just lost it. I raised my hand to her, Maddie."

"But you didn't hit her."

He shook his head. "I wanted to. Instead I knocked a hole in the wall. Then I packed up and left. I don't ever want to feel that way again. I'm telling you a regular life like I had with her isn't for me."

"It isn't for me, either," Maddie said quietly.

He stared at her. "You're just saying that."

"It isn't!" Why wouldn't he believe her? "It doesn't matter whether you go or stay, but I'm not staying here. I can't. I've had it with trying to be someone I'm not, and I can understand the crazy feeling you get. I think I'd like your life, but not on your terms—my terms." Maddie drew a deep breath. "I love you. You don't have to say anything back. I just wanted you to know."

The hardest thing she'd ever done was to walk off and leave him standing in the darkened hallway.

SHE LOVED HIM. It was more than he deserved.

He drew a deep shuddering breath. She loved him. In spite of it all, she loved him. But he'd known, hadn't he? Maddie wasn't the type of woman to give herself to someone she didn't love.

And now she'd offered to share his life on her terms. He didn't even know what those terms were.

"Maddie?" he called after her, but she was gone.

He walked through the rec room, stopping to help

Gloria glue the support to the stable roof back together.

"Have you seen Maddie?" he asked, not sure of his reception.

"With the angels and lambs in a room off that hallway," Gloria answered with a smile that told him Maddie hadn't discussed the other night with her sister.

Thanking Gloria, he avoided Preacher Given's eyes and found Maddie in a small nursery.

She was trying to line up the sheep, but Luke was giving her fits.

Steve walked across the room and held out his arms for the baby.

Maddie eyed him warily, but handed Luke to him.

"What terms?" Steve asked, putting Luke over his shoulder.

Maddie gave him a direct and unapologetic look. "Marriage."

He had to tamp down a little residual echo of panic before asking, "That's it?"

Maddie appeared to consider. "Marriage and a motorcycle. I want to be able to travel with you."

He was lost, and he knew it. He suspected Maddie knew it, too. "You never say what I think you're going to say."

Her smile was brief and matter of fact. "Think it over. I've got sheep to herd."

Luke was still fussy. Maddie nodded to the diaper bag on a child-sized chair. "He usually likes his sock puppets. Maybe with your voice, it'll calm him."

Sock puppets. One minute they were talking marriage and motorcycles, the next, he was digging in a diaper bag for sock puppets.

And the thing was, he didn't even mind.

It felt right. Very, very right.

Steve set Luke on his knees and talked to him as he pulled out a puppet and put it on.

"And who's this?" He turned the puppet to face Luke. The baby stopped fussing and reached for the puppet.

"That's Harry Yellow Eyes," Maddie called.

Steve made the puppet mouth, "I'm Harry Yellow Eyes." He turned the puppet toward himself. "Now why are you called...?"

Steve stared at the puppet, the puppet with the gold button eyes. His heart skipped a beat. "Maddie, come here."

Something in his voice must have alerted her, because she left her sheep and knelt down beside him. "What is it?"

At the sight of her concerned face, everything became clear. "A couple of things. First, I love you," Steve told her, getting his priorities right. "And I want you on any terms. But Maddie, if you like, could we maybe have one of these one day?" He gestured to the baby in his lap.

"I like." Her voice was a broken whisper.

"I want to get it right this time. Help me?"

She nodded and sniffed.

They weren't exactly private, or Steve would be kissing her right now. He might anyway.

"What was the second thing?" she asked.

"Does Harry, here, have a brother, by chance?"

Maddie's eyes were bright, but she nodded. "A

twin—Larry Yellow Eyes." She pulled another sock puppet out of the diaper bag.

Luke gurgled and stretched his arms toward them.

"You've got great taste, kid." He showed the puppets to Maddie. "They should be called the golden-eyed brothers, don't you think?"

He held the puppets out, waiting for realization to strike.

Her eyes widened. "The doubloons?"

"In person."

"But how did they get there?"

"Maddie?" Gloria appeared in the doorway. "We fixed the sets and we're going to start the program now."

"Gloria, where did you get these buttons?"

She came over and picked up Luke, then her mouth opened in an O of distress. "I forgot! Those were on the jacket the two men wanted. John thought the jacket was too flashy, so I replaced those buttons with navy blue ones. Oh, I hope the men aren't too upset."

"I believe they're just happy to have the jacket back," Steve reassured her.

"Good." Gloria's smile returned. "Thanks for watching Luke. I'll go tell Mother that we're ready."

Steve stared at the sock puppets, scarcely able to believe what he held.

"So," Maddie said. "Your work here is done." She wasn't meeting his eyes.

"Mostly." What was the matter? "I'll arrange for your sister and brother-in-law to receive the finders' fee," Steve offered.

"Will it be a lot?" She sounded like it didn't matter.

He did a quick calculation. "Thousands."

Maddie nodded. "They'll give it to the center."

"Maybe they'd like to start college funds for the kids."

"Maybe."

Steve tilted her chin until he could see her eyes.

"I guess this means you'll be leaving again," she said, her voice strained.

He smiled gently at her. "I told you I loved you."

"I know, but—"

"I told you I accept your terms," he interrupted.

"I know, but—"

"So, yes, Maddie, I'm leaving—but this time, I'm taking you with me."

Her smile was luminous and Steve felt like he was coming home at last.

"One favor?" she asked.

"Name it."

"Can we wait until after the Christmas pageant?"

What a woman. "Long after. I understand there's a big turkey dinner here tomorrow. I wouldn't want to miss that."

"Oh, Steve!"

Maddie looked like she was about to cry, so in front of the lambs and angels, Steve kissed her. He didn't know whether it helped, or not, but it sure as he—heck, sure as heck—made him feel better.

"They're singing the shepherd song, Aunt Maddie!" Matt shrieked.

"I've got to take them in." She started for the door, then turned back. "You'll wait here?"

"I'm coming with you," Steve told her. "I don't want to go anywhere without you ever again."

HARLEQUIN® Temptation.

When times are tough, and good men are hard to find... who are you going to call?

FANTASY FOR HIRE

**Temptation #759 *CHRISTMAS FANTASY*
by Janelle Denison
On sale November 1999**

Fulfilling women's fantasies was Austin McBride's business. But his gorgeous client, Teddy Spencer, had Austin doing some fantasizing of his own....

**Temptation #767 *VALENTINE FANTASY*
by Jamie Denton
On sale January 2000**

Reporter Cait Sullivan was determined to expose Fantasy for Hire, even if it meant going undercover. But once she met sexy-as-sin Jordan McBride, all she could think about was getting him "under the covers"...

Fantasy for Hire
Your pleasure is our business!

Available at your favorite retail outlet.

HARLEQUIN®
Makes any time special ™

Visit us at www.romance.net

HTFFH

If you enjoyed what you just read,
then we've got an offer you can't resist!

Take 2 bestselling love stories FREE!

Plus get a FREE surprise gift!

Temptation®

COMING NEXT MONTH

EXTRA! EXTRA!

The book all your favorite authors are raving about is finally here!

The 1999 Harlequin and Silhouette coupon book.

Each page is alive with savings that can't be beat!

Getting this incredible coupon book is as easy as 1, 2, 3.

1. During the months of November and December 1999 buy any 2 Harlequin or Silhouette books.

2. Send us your name, address and 2 proofs of purchase (cash receipt) to the address below.

3. Harlequin will send you a coupon book worth $10.00 off future purchases of Harlequin or Silhouette books in 2000.

Send us 3 cash register receipts as proofs of purchase and we will send you 2 coupon books worth a total saving of $20.00 (limit of 2 coupon books per customer).

Saving money has never been this easy.

Please allow 4-6 weeks for delivery. Offer expires December 31, 1999.

I accept your offer! Please send me (a) coupon booklet(s):

Name: _____

Address: _____ City: _____

State/Prov.: _____ Zip/Postal Code: _____

Send your name and address, along with your cash register receipts as proofs of purchase, to:

In the U.S.: Harlequin Books, P.O. Box 9057, Buffalo, N.Y. 14269

In Canada: Harlequin Books, P.O. Box 622, Fort Erie, Ontario L2A 5X3

Order your books and accept this coupon offer through our web site
http://www.romance.net
Valid in U.S. and Canada only.

PHQ4994R